BOOKS BY PHYLLIS REYNOLDS NAYLOR

Witch's Sister
Witch Water
The Witch Herself
Walking Through the Dark
How I Came to Be a Writer
How Lazy Can You Get?
Eddie, Incorporated
All Because I'm Older
Shadows on the Wall
Faces in the Water
Footprints at the Window
The Boy With the Helium Head
A String of Chances
The Solomon System
The Mad Gasser of Bessledorf Street
Night Cry
Old Sadie and the Christmas Bear
The Dark of the Tunnel
The Agony of Alice
The Keeper

The Keeper

The
Keeper

Phyllis Reynolds Naylor

Atheneum   1986   New York

Lyrics from
"Cat's in the Cradle" by Harry Chapin,
© 1974 by Story Songs,
reprinted by permission of the Chapin estate.

With special thanks to
Jon and Marilyn Hinton.

Library of Congress Cataloging-in-Publication Data

Naylor, Phyllis Reynolds.   The keeper.

SUMMARY: *Junior high school student Nick must*
face the fact that his father is plunging fast
into serious mental illness.
[1. Mentally ill—Fiction.   2. Fathers—Fiction]
I. Title.
PZ7.N24Ke 1986   [Fic]   85-20029
ISBN 0-689-31204-0

Copyright © 1986 by Phyllis Reynolds Naylor
All rights reserved
Published simultaneously in Canada by
Collier Macmillan Canada, Inc.
Composition by Maryland Linotype, Baltimore, Maryland
Printed and bound by
Fairfield Graphics, Fairfield, Pennsylvania
Designed by Mary Ahern
First Edition

To HENRY MYERS
with affection and gratitude

The Keeper

One

THE SWIRLING SNOW could not reach him beneath the underpass. Nick still felt the wind from Lake Michigan pushing against his back, however. Above him, the el slid to a stop with a noise like a roller coaster making a dip, then moved on. As Nick walked out the other side, the snow sprayed steadily against his cheek.

He crossed at the light, icy flakes seeping down into his sneakers. Here the snow was discolored by tire tracks and exhaust. When he was small, Nick used to think of it as brown sugar. It didn't seem like sugar anymore.

Past the Golden Buddha carryout, the dry-cleaning shop, Walgreens, the deli, and then St. John's. A row of apartment buildings loomed up on his right, apartments as far as the eye could see. Nick shifted his books to the other arm. Biology and

English to do that night—only an hour's worth, maybe. Might be time enough later to go to the Y and shoot some baskets.

Discarded Christmas trees lay propped against garbage cans along the curb, waiting for tomorrow's pickup, little bits of tinsel trapped in the needles. When he was four and they lived in Logansport, Nick would drag all the old Christmas trees into his own yard to make a cave, then sit hidden in their branches, drunk with the scent of pine. There was no cave to crawl in now.

Schmidt, the building superintendent, was shoveling the walk. He straightened up, rubbing the small of his back, when Nick approached.

"I *used* to like this stuff," he said, smiling.

"Getting deep?" Nick asked.

"Naw. Weather stays this cold, though, it'll be around for a while."

Rows of mailboxes lined one wall of the entryway. *J. Karpinski, 307*, one read. Nick peered through the slit into the blackness. Dad must have gotten the mail already.

He went through the second set of doors into the lobby, with its cold gray pillars, tracks of wet shoes on the tiled floor. Through the doors on the other side, he could see the small circle of park behind the building, its evergreens snow-shrouded. Nick started up the stairs.

By the time he reached the first landing he could

hear it, "The Spinning Wheel Song": da da da da da . . . *da* . . . da *da*; da da da da da . . . *da* . . . da *da*. . . . He went on up. There were only two apartments per floor from this stairway, and when Nick reached the third, he entered the apartment on the right.

A blond girl of ten was sitting on a chair against the wall. She had left her boots by the door and was swinging her stockinged feet in time to the music coming from the study. She smiled shyly when Nick walked in.

"Hi," he said.

"Hi." She dropped her eyes and continued swinging her feet.

The coffee table was covered with old copies of *Highlights for Children*, *Jack and Jill*. A small boy's parka was draped over one arm of the couch.

"Watch your fingering here," came Mother's voice from the study. "Try this measure again."

Da da da da da . . . *da* . . . da *da*. . . .

Nick went down the hall to his room and tossed his books on the bed. The floorboards creaked behind him and he turned to see his father standing there in the doorway.

Jacob Karpinski was a large-boned man, square chin, big ears. *Craggy-looking*, Mother had always said of him and Nick, and said it with affection. Behind horn-rimmed glasses, Jacob's eyes were intense.

"You see a man down there when you came in?" he asked.

Nick took off his jacket. "Yeah. Mr. Schmidt."

"Schmidt, huh?" His father waited. "You sure it was Schmidt?"

"Of course I'm sure. I was talking to him."

Mr. Karpinski walked over to Nick's window and looked down at the street below. His shoulders were hunched, like those of a large cat. A car door slammed somewhere down the block, and Nick's father jerked his head, staring out the window in the other direction. Then he turned and wordlessly left the room. Nick could hear him pacing back and forth in the bedroom next to his.

He sat down on the edge of his bed, hands dangling loosely between his knees. A hollowness ballooned inside him, and when he let out his breath, it came shakily. There was no way to transport himself back in time to those pine-scented days in a snowy yard or forward five years to college—no way he could get out of living through whatever was going to happen next.

I T H A D all started with Christmas. A week before, actually. Nick came home from school to find his father there.

"What are you doing home so early?" he'd asked casually. But Jacob didn't answer.

Nick had gone into the study between pupils and

6

confronted his mother, who stood leafing through sheet music beside the piano. She was a slim woman, almost as tall as her husband, and on that particular day seemed as delicate as the papers she was fingering.

"What's with Dad?" Nick had asked.

Her gray eyes looked over at him quickly, then dropped to the music again.

"Jacob may have lost his job, Nick."

"What?" Nick lowered himself down on the piano bench. "What happened?"

"I don't know. That's all he'll tell me."

There had been other jobs in other cities, but they were always preceded by an announcement from Jacob; it was always a step up, he said, a better deal, and Nick had become used to only two or three years in one place before they moved on again. In South Bend, however, Jacob had gone back to college to become an insurance actuary and had studied hard for a job with Life Trust. Nick still remembered the excitement in his father's face when he announced he was being transferred to Chicago. They had all been excited, Mother too. Maybe this time, she'd said to Nick, they'd stay put.

Nick continued staring at his mother. "Was he fired, Mom?"

"I can't get any more out of him, Nick. Maybe later, after all the students have gone. . . ."

Later, however, Jacob had been no more communicative. Their interrogation at supper only made him snappish, and his answers seemed hardly answers at all. Nick had listened in disbelief. It was as though there were a larger problem that absorbed his father, something far more ominous than his job. Jacob couldn't sit still, couldn't even stand in one place, and finally they had all gone to bed, the questioners and the questioned, equally exhausted. The next day was the same, and the next and the next.

It was, Nick thought, as if a stranger had moved into the apartment and into his father's clothes. Where the old Jacob had been meticulous and precise, the new Jacob Karpinski left papers strewn about the living room, letters unopened, bills unpaid. The man who had always risen at a certain time each morning, even on weekends, and gone through a seven-minute shaving ritual, now went days at a time without shaving at all. Before, Nick's father had been as dependable as a railway schedule. Each time they moved and he took a new job, it was Jacob who found another apartment for them, a new school for Nick; Jacob who carefully researched the bus schedules and located the public library. No one could balance the checkbook like Nick's father, make out the income tax as thoroughly, keep the records on the car or even drive it as carefully. Mother didn't even try. There was no need. Jacob did it all. Who was this stranger who had taken his place?

But Christmas had come in spite of Jacob Karpinski. Nick kept the radio on most of the time, flooding the apartment with carols, filling up the silence. In a sudden flurry of activity, his father had gone shopping the day before and returned home with an armload of gifts—expensive gifts. Nick could tell by the names of the stores on the boxes. Jacob had insisted, strangely, on showing Nick and his mother what he had bought for them, as though tomorrow might be too late. He seemed affectionate, anxious, and melancholy in turn. Mrs. Karpinski wrapped the gifts herself and placed them under the tree with the rest.

Nick's grandparents drove over from Hammond on Christmas Day—Grandpa and Grandma Rycek. Nick could hear them puffing on the stairs—making a big deal of four flights, the way they always did. They stopped on the second landing to call out, "Hoo! Hoo! Anyone home?" and Nick went down to help carry up their packages. They were in a good mood, laughing and joshing with each other.

"I brought your favorite," Grandma said to Nick, handing him a bag of homemade doughnuts. "And for your mother, something special." She winked.

"Chruscik!" Nick's mother cried when she saw the pastries. "Mama, you've been baking all week!"

And then all eyes turned to Jacob, who came to the door smiling stiffly, shook hands, and went back to staring out the window.

It was a strange Christmas. Gifts were opened

mechanically, with exclamations of exaggerated delight. And between each gift were the silences—awkward and uncomfortable.

When Nick and his mother went out in the kitchen to prepare the relish tray, Grandma Rycek came too.

"Wanda, what on earth is wrong?" she asked quietly.

Nick waited for the answer, wanting to see if the problem could be put into words, if the frustration and helplessness of the past few days could be condensed, somehow, into sentences. And then he heard his mother say, "Jacob's having some problems at work, Mama. We'll just have to let him work things out his own way."

Nick stared at her, but Mother held her chin high as she turned to get a platter from the cupboard. Even here with Grandma she held onto pride tightly, as though it were the only thing to keep them all from sinking. "Just let him be—don't try to pull him into the conversation. He's going through a difficult time, that's all."

Grandma Rycek looked at her with questioning eyes but did not ask the question, and when she carried the relishes into the other room, Nick said, "Mom, we're not even sure Dad *has* a job anymore. Can't we even tell *her*?"

"Wait till there's something to tell," Mother had answered. "I can't believe that Jacob won't get his job back. He's simply too intelligent to let a good job like that slip away from him."

Dinner was difficult. Twice Jacob had to be reminded to come to the table and, once there, could not seem to concentrate on the conversation around him. He left to get the coffeepot and when he didn't return, Nick went into the kitchen to find him staring out the back window into the alley below. The platters of food were passed around the table once and then sat undisturbed for the rest of the meal.

"Well," said Grandpa at last, holding up his wine glass. "Perhaps next year will be better. To the new year. . . ."

"To the new year," the family repeated, and clinked their glasses, Jacob's included. But Nick's father put his glass down again without drinking and sat distracted while the others finished.

Last year at this time, Nick was thinking, his father and grandfather had been absorbed in a new video game on Nick's Atari, and afterwards Mother and Grandpa had played a mazurka for four hands on the piano.

"Three-fourths time, Papa!" Wanda Karpinski laughed as their fingers stumbled across the keys. And when their hands collided at last and they stopped, breathless, Jacob had quipped:

"How many Poles does it take to play Chopin?"

"Five!" called out Grandma Rycek. "Two to play, two to listen, and one to make such smart remarks."

There were carols after that, and though Jacob hadn't sung, he'd watched from the sidelines and seemed to be enjoying himself. How could his father have changed so much in only one year's time? Nick wondered.

There had been carols this year too, but no one sang, and after a few minutes, Mother pushed away from the piano.

Out in the hall, Mrs. Karpinski had told her parents goodbye and Nick saw tears in her eyes as she hugged her father, noticed the unfamiliar tremble of her narrow chin.

"Let us know, Wanda," her father said earnestly, his hands on his daughter's shoulders. "Good or bad, we want to hear."

Nick's mother nodded.

In the week that followed, however, there had been nothing to tell because nothing changed. Every day Nick woke anticipating some decision on his father's part, some action—an explanation, at the very least. But each day was the same as the one before. Jacob never left the apartment, and at last Mrs. Karpinski went to the drugstore on the corner to call her parents in private and say that nothing had changed.

"What's he going to do, Mom? Just bum around the apartment for the rest of his life?" Nick had asked one morning, and his mother whirled about, answering sharply:

12

"Don't you ever speak like that about him again, Nick."

"Well, what's going to happen to us? I'm worried about you too, Mom."

"In a few weeks, if he's not over this, I'll decide then what to do. Don't keep at me. I've got worries enough."

"Why don't we just call his office and find out what happened?"

"*No*, Nick! Do you want them to know he hasn't told us himself?"

Perhaps that's what really hurt—that they felt so excluded. Not that Jacob had ever been particularly close and confiding, but at least Nick had always felt they were a team, he and his parents. If Nick ever had a problem, he felt sure, his father would go over every possible solution with him until they had found one that would work. Now that Jacob had problems, however, he kept them all in.

When school started again in January, Nick fell into his old routine. Outside the apartment, at least, things went on much as they always had. He walked to his eighth-grade classes each morning a half block behind Karen Zimmerman who lived in the west wing of his apartment building. He always paced himself so he didn't catch up with her, partly because he liked to watch the way she wove in and out among people on the sidewalk, her reddish hair swirling from under her stocking cap, and partly because Danny Beck had his eye on Karen and Nick didn't want to blow it for Danny. Mostly, however, it was because Nick hadn't the slightest idea what he would say if he ever caught up with her.

Christmas decorations were packed away and the old issues of children's magazines took their place on the coffee table once again. The piano students returned to the Karpinski apartment for lessons between three and six on weekdays and twelve and four on Saturdays. But back in the far bedroom, Jacob Karpinski kept up his steady pacing, and to Nick, it seemed the drum beat of some secret ritual, known only to his father.

THE BIOLOGY and English assignments took less than an hour.

"I'm going to shoot some baskets at the Y," Nick said at the dinner table.

"Good. I worry you're not getting enough exercise—so closed up like this in the winter," his mother told him, and Nick knew that she was speaking to Jacob as well.

Nick's father sat chewing absently as though he could not even taste the food. He put down his fork, cracked the knuckles on his left hand with his right, then resumed eating again.

"Jacob," said Mrs. Karpinski, "why don't you go shoot baskets with Nick? Remember how you used to do that?"

14

Jacob smiled as if to himself. "You'd like that, wouldn't you?"

Nick felt a lump of potato go halfway down his throat and stop. He swallowed.

"Of course I would like that!" his mother said. "I would like to see you getting out, doing something with yourself."

Jacob stopped smiling and silently hunched over his coffee again.

"Well, *I'm* going," Nick said at last, scooting away from the table. He looked across at his father. "You want to come or not?"

"No. I'm not going."

"Suit yourself."

Nick walked to the phone in the kitchen and lifted the receiver.

"Who you calling?" asked his father.

"Danny." Nick waited. Jacob made no reply, so he dialed the number.

There was something enormously reassuring about the telephone—a safety line, connecting Nick to people on the outside. When his friend answered, Nick asked, "Want to shoot some baskets?"

"Yeah, but I've got to finish a Spanish assignment first," Danny told him. "Why don't you come by in a half hour?"

"See you then."

Nick put on his sweat jacket and pants and took the ball downstairs. He preferred to wait there rather than in the apartment. Standing in the foyer between the outer and inner doors, he dribbled the ball a few times around the tiled floor. Out of the corner of his eye, he saw Karen Zimmerman crossing the lobby. Then she was opening the door to the foyer, humming to herself—a sort of self-conscious, buzzlike hum, with her lips apart—the way she did when Nick passed her in the corridor at school.

"Pretty small court, isn't it?" She laughed.

Nick smiled, embarrassed. "Just waiting around," he mumbled. "I'm going over to the Y later with Danny."

Karen took her mittens from her pockets and slipped them on. "How was Christmas?"

With all the sociability he could muster, Nick told her, "Fantastic. Really great. How about yours?"

"Uh . . . well, we don't celebrate Christmas."

Nick's stomach took a dive. "Jeez, I'm so stupid."

She laughed. "We had a nice Hanukkah. How's that?"

He smiled, still blushing.

"Tell Danny I said hello," she added, and went out, almost colliding with someone coming in. The man carried a box in his arms, and Nick held the door open so it wouldn't slam against him, then opened the inner doors.

"Thanks. Say, aren't you Jacob Karpinski's son?"

Nick recognized one of the men from his father's car pool.

16

"Hello, Mr. Edmunds. I wasn't sure it was you under that cap."

The man smiled and paused there in the doorway. "Listen, could I talk to you for a minute?"

"Sure." Nick felt his spine stiffen as he followed him inside.

Mr. Edmunds set the open box on a narrow table in the lobby. "We thought your dad would be back to clean out his desk. I finally decided to bring his things by. If there's anything else he's left around the office, I'll be glad to run it over. This is all I could find."

Nick struggled against the question he wanted to ask. Mr. Edmunds stood staring down at the floor, lips pressed together, rocking back and forth on his heels.

"Took us all by surprise, you know. We figured something was bothering him that last week, but had no idea he'd just walk out like that."

Nick did not move. Mr. Edmunds' words went ricocheting around in his brain, but Nick himself scarcely breathed. He waited. Mr. Edmunds waited.

"I don't know what the trouble was," Mr. Edmunds said finally, "but what I think is he should come in and have a talk with the manager—no hard feelings. Just get it off his chest. We all go through rough times now and then, and Connelly's got heart. He'd understand; he'd listen. He's hired someone else, but he could find another place in the company for Jacob. I think your dad's got to make the first move, though. Can't just walk off the job like that without a word to anyone."

Nick nodded woodenly.

"Listen . . ." Mr. Edmunds clapped one gloved hand on Nick's shoulder. "I've got to run—parked by a fire hydrant. I'd sure appreciate it if you'd take the box up for me. Give it to your father. Tell him what I said. He's got to make the first move. Okay?" He patted Nick's shoulder again, and then, looking relieved, walked quickly out to the street.

Nick scanned the contents of the box. *Jacob Karpinski*, read a walnut nameplate with gold letters. There were pens, papers, a leather in-box, a coffee mug, a stainless steel tape dispenser. And down in one corner, in a narrow wood frame, a photo of Nick and his mother, taken four years ago on a trip to the Smokies. Nick picked up the picture and studied their faces.

Mrs. Karpinski, dressed in blouse and jodhpurs, sat on a tree stump, a wide, relaxed smile on her face. Nick stood behind her, one hand on a branch above. Anyone passing his father's desk must have thought, looking at the picture, *Now there's a happy family.*

And they had been once. Maybe Nick hadn't been as close to his father as Danny Beck was to his, but Jacob Karpinski was a private person, that's all. A very private person.

The odd part was that the man his father had become—the stranger—had a vague sense of the familiar about him. The silences, the looks, the restlessness, however unusual, seemed at times mere exaggerations of traits that had been a part of Jacob's personality as far back as Nick could remember. Maybe the problem had not started at Christmas or even the week before, but a long time ago, and Nick had never noticed.

Two

R U B B E R S O L E S squeaked on the hardwood floor as Nick and Danny pounded down the court with the other boys. There was always a crowd, but it was easier to talk your way into a game if there were two of you than if you tried to do it alone. Nick was usually too shy to even try.

Arms reaching, knees bending, bodies twisting. . . . Droplets of perspiration rolled off Nick's face. Here he was an anonymous member of a team, disconnected from the apartment and whatever was happening at home.

He shot for a basket, hit the backboard, and missed—retrieved the ball, shot again, and made it. Each time, he was throwing off that ten-pound weight of worry, and for a while he almost lost it. Even when the game was over and he felt worry settle down on his shoulders again, it did not seem quite so heavy.

"Come on over," Danny invited as they left the gym. "We can watch TV, throw in a pizza . . ."

A steamy smell of chlorine greeted them in the corridor, the echoed shouts of swimmers, the splash of water, the thunk of the diving board. . . . Whenever they passed the indoor pool it reminded Nick of peppermints—of being back in third grade when they lived in Lafayette and taking swimming lessons at the local Y after school. Jacob Karpinski would come to pick up his son and always had peppermints in his pocket.

Nick braced himself against the cold as they went out a side door and started toward the lighted boulevard.

"Saw Karen as I was leaving tonight. Said to tell you hello," Nick mentioned.

"Yeah? She say anything else about me?"

"No, but she sounded friendly. Why don't you ask her out."

"I'm thinking about it."

Nick smiled to himself. *Yeah, I'll bet,* he thought. Danny was as inexperienced as he was. He might not be as shy as Nick, but he sure wasn't any Casanova.

They followed a narrow path through the park, stomped the snow off their sneakers on the other side, and cut across traffic to Danny's apartment building. And then Danny said, "Why don't you ask Lois Mueller and we'll go together?"

Nick immediately colored. "Who said I was interested in Lois?"

"Oh, come on!" Danny punched him in the shoulder. "I saw you looking at her in study hall."

The Beck apartment smelled of roast beef from supper. Danny's parents, both short and heavy, with curly hair like their son's, were leaving for a movie.

"Enjoy the holidays, Nick?" Mr. Beck asked.

"Great. Really fantastic. Hard to get back in the old grind." Nick knew the words now for *sounding* sociable, even when he didn't feel it inside.

Danny's mother pulled on her coat. "Yes, but isn't it nice to be upperclassmen this year? In high school you'll have to start at the bottom again. Enjoy it while you can."

Danny found a sausage pizza in the freezer, and ten minutes later, the boys ate it half-baked with a bottle of Pepsi. As the last bite of crust disappeared, Danny wiped one hand over his lips and slapped the table. "Okay," he said. "Let's call the girls."

Nick stared at him in horror. "You're serious!"

"Of course."

"What do I say?"

Danny considered it for a moment. He didn't seem so sure himself. "Look. I'll call Lois and pretend I'm you, and you call Karen and say you're me.

Then, if they hang up or something, it won't be so bad."

Nick gave a startled laugh. "You're *nuts*, Danny."

"You got a better idea? Ask her out on Saturday night. We'll double—a movie or something."

"Oh, jeez, I don't know. . . ."

"What's the worst that can happen? If she says no and hangs up on you, you don't have to do anything."

"What if she says no and *doesn't* hang up?"

"Listen. If she says she's got to do homework, that's a no. Then you just say, 'Well, some other time.' Got it?"

"What if she's going away?"

"That's a maybe. If she sounds sincere, ask about the Saturday after that."

"You go first," said Nick.

Danny reached around for the telephone directory and looked up Lois Mueller's number. He held one finger on the place.

"Don't make me sound like a nerd," said Nick. "Ask her about the biology assignment first. Ask what pages we were supposed to read."

Danny stood up, dialed the number from the phone on the wall, then sat down again and tipped back his chair.

"Hello, is Lois there? . . . Lois Mueller? . . . Oh. Sorry." Danny reached up and clicked the phone behind him. "Wrong number," he said. Nick closed his eyes.

Danny checked the number again, stood up and dialed, sat back down.

"Hello? Lois? . . . Hi. This is Nick Karpinski. How you doing? . . . Yeah. . . . Nick, from biology class." Danny spread his knees, propping his feet on the side rungs of the chair. "Yeah . . . yeah. . . . You finished already? Well, that's what I was calling about. I wondered what pages we were supposed to read. . . . Right. Got it."

There was a pause and Danny fidgeted around with the telephone cord. Nick could feel his own face growing warm.

"Say, Lois, I was wondering . . . would you be interested in seeing a movie this Saturday? . . . Well, we could make it the Saturday after if you're not sure. . . ."

Nick watched without breathing.

"Well, I was thinking maybe we could go with Danny Beck and Karen Zimmerman. . . . No, I don't think he's asked her yet, but I could let you know. . . . What? . . . Of course I'm Nick Karpinski. . . ! Yeah, well, I've got sort of a cold. . . . Okay, we'll make it a week from Saturday, and I'll let you know later what time. See you."

Smirking, Danny reached to hang up the phone but missed and the receiver thunked against the wall. Nick dived for it and replaced it on the hook.

"Yahoo!" Danny yelled. "You've got yourself a date!"

"She knew we were pulling something, didn't she?" said Nick, mortified.

"Listen, she said yes. What more do you want? Now call Karen."

"Maybe she's not home yet."

"So try!"

Nick looked up the number and lifted the receiver. The telephone had suddenly taken on frightening dimensions. Even the dial tone sounded ominous. If anyone had told him back in South Bend that he'd be doing something like this—Nick Karpinski, the shy kid with the big feet—Nick would have thought he was crazy.

"Busy," he said with relief, and hung up. "Tell me everything Lois said. Did she sound as though she really wanted to go?"

"Why would she say so if she didn't?"

"How come she couldn't go out this Saturday?"

"Thinks her aunt and uncle may be coming. Go ahead—try Karen's number again."

Nick dialed again, sure that the line would still be busy. He heard a ring at the other end and swallowed.

"Hello?" It was a man's voice, deep and gravel-sounding.

"Is Karen Zimmerman there?" *Why in the world did he say her last name?* Nick saw Danny wince.

"Just a minute," said the voice.

"Hello?" It was Karen, all right.

"Uh . . . This is Danny Beck."

There seemed an unnatural pause at the other end.

"Danny? I thought you were over at the Y with Nick."

"I was, but I'm home now."

Across the table, Danny was motioning downward with the palm of his hand, pointing to his throat with the other hand.

"How was Christmas?" Karen was asking.

Nick concentrated on lowering his voice a little. "Really fantastic. How was yours?"

The color drained suddenly from his face and Nick let his arms drop, the receiver still in his hand. Danny lunged from his chair and thrust the receiver back against Nick's ear, his eyes frantic.

". . . but we had a nice Hanukkuh," Karen was saying.

"Oh, sure," Nick recovered. "I meant Hanukkuh."

There was silence. His palms began to sweat. The phone felt slippery in his hand.

"I was wondering if you'd like to go out a week from Saturday—take in a movie or something," he said at last.

"Naturally."

Nick stared at Danny. *Naturally?* What was he supposed to say to "naturally"?

Danny's face looked tortured with uncertainty.

"You . . . you would?" Nick said at last.

Karen's voice was laughing. "I said so, didn't I?"

"Well, great! Terrific!" (Danny pranced delightedly around the table, a fist raised in triumph). "I thought maybe we could go with Nick Karpinski and Lois Mueller."

Karen's voice was still laughing. "Has Nick asked her?"

"Yeah. She said yes."

"That's settled, then."

"I guess so. Fine. Swell. I'll call later and let you know what time."

When the receiver was back on the hook, the boys sprawled on the kitchen chairs once more, smiling stupidly at each other, and spent the rest of the evening dissecting the girls' answers word by word until, the subject exhausted, they turned on the TV.

But Nick was thinking of what lay ahead—of what the four of them could do together if things worked out. He imagined them all coming back to Danny's apartment after the movie and making a pizza. He imagined it very well. Then he thought of them going back to the Karpinskis' apartment and fooling around on the piano. And suddenly the picture stopped, the characters froze, and Nick found he could not imagine it at all.

*　*　*

ACTUALLY, Nick had not given the box to his
father. After Mr. Edmunds left, Nick had gone upstairs, cautiously opened the door as though it led
to a lion's cage, and thrust the box in the hall closet.
He had not wanted a hassle with his dad just then.
Danny would be waiting.

When he came home later, however, he walked
in to find the box on the coffee table, papers
scattered on the floor, his father agitated, his mother
distraught.

"Nick," she said, "how did these things get in
here?"

He had made a mistake, Nick realized. No matter
what he did with his father, though, it was a mistake.

"I ran into Mr. Edmunds as I was leaving for the
Y and he gave me this stuff to give to Dad."

"Yeah?" Jacob said. "Yeah? You and Edmunds,
huh?"

"What?" Nick took off his sweat jacket and
stared at him.

"Hiding things from me, doing things behind my
back."

"What are you talking about, Dad? I just didn't
want a lot of questions. I had to get over to Danny's.
I was going to give it to you when I got back. What's
the big deal?"

"Well, what did Mr. Edmunds say, Nick?"

28

Mother looked at Nick imploringly, as though he had within him the secret of this whole nutty business.

"He said that when Dad didn't come back to clean out his desk, he decided to bring the stuff over himself. He said this was all he could find, but if there was anything else, let him know."

"That's all?" Mrs. Karpinski asked incredulously. "Just like that? 'Here are Jacob's things'?"

Like a drumbeat, Nick's heart began to pick up tempo. "No, he said something else: he said everyone is wondering why Dad just walked off the job without saying anything to anybody."

Mrs. Karpinski's lips parted. She stared at Nick, then at her husband. Jacob smiled faintly and walked over to the window, nervously cracking his knuckles.

"Listen, Dad," Nick went on, "I don't know what happened at work, but Mr. Edmunds said he thinks they'd take you back if you talked to Mr. Connelly."

"See, Jacob? Just a misunderstanding!" Mother interrupted nervously.

"He said that you've got to make the first move, though, that it was up to you to go to him."

"The first move, huh? What did he mean by that?" Jacob asked.

"I don't *understand*!" Mother turned from Nick to Jacob and back to Nick again.

"*They* know why I left," Jacob said, as if to the

tree outside, the window. "Well, maybe Bill Edmunds doesn't—he's okay; he can't help himself, just does what he's told—but Connelly knows."

"Knows *what*, Jacob?" his wife begged. "Why all this secrecy? You had me thinking something awful had happened at work. I thought they'd fired you!"

"What difference does it make?" Jacob shot back, the agitation playing on his face once more. "If I kept working there, you know how I'd come home? In a box. I know. I know the signs. That's what Edmunds was trying to tell me—that's why he brought the things in a box. I'm not so dumb."

Nick could scarcely believe what he was hearing.

Jacob came back to the coffee table and—as Nick and his mother watched—began to examine the box carefully. He turned it upside down, dumping the remaining papers out on the rug. The photo of Nick and his mother in the wood and glass frame hit the edge of the table and cracked, but Jacob did not even seem to notice. He tore open the bottom flaps of the box and checked beneath them, until there was nothing left but a flattened piece of cardboard.

"What are you doing?" Nick asked. "What are you looking for, Dad? You act like you're crazy!"

Jacob's eyes were like dark buttons beneath his thick brows. "That's what Bill told you, huh? Your dad's crazy?"

"No! He didn't say anything like that! How come you're trying to turn everything around?" Nick was surprised at the way his voice shook, whether from fear or anger, he couldn't tell.

"You'll find out in good time," his father said, dropping the broken box to the floor. "We'll all find out. The only way Jacob Karpinski's going to get out of Chicago is in a box. That's the way they want it."

"*Who*, Jacob? *Who* wants it?" Nick's mother said, her voice suddenly shrill. "Are you saying that someone is trying to kill you?"

"If I told you, you'd never believe me," Jacob said, suddenly looking more tired than Nick had ever seen him—like an old man, almost. Then he left the room.

Nick turned to his mother. She was leaning back against the sofa cushions, eyes closed, tears showing under the lashes. Nick sat helplessly down beside her, not knowing what to say that would be comforting to either of them.

"Mom," he said finally, "you think he's in some kind of trouble?"

She cried. "He'll tell me, Nick. I'm sure he will."

"Listen." Nick tried to be gentle. "We've got to find out. Call Mr. Connelly yourself and ask him. Maybe he knows."

"I would *never* do that, Nick! *Never!*" Mrs. Karpinski stood up, her blouse spotted with tears, and went across the room for a tissue. "We aren't saying *anything* to *anybody*! Don't you realize how humiliating this is? Even Bill Edmunds knows more than I do."

"Well, *I* want to find out what's happened," Nick said. "I don't want to go off to school every day wondering what I'm going to find when I get home."

Mrs. Karpinski blew her nose. "What you'll find is me giving piano lessons, just like always," she said. "We're a family, Nick, and we're still together. If *you* were having some kind of problem, we'd stick by you."

"Mom, I'm not talking about sticking together. I'm just trying to find out what's going on. Maybe someone could help! You won't even tell Grandpa about it."

"Papa's an old man. There's not a thing he can do but worry."

"Uncle Thad, then."

"I've never been close to Thad, you know that, Nick. But if I have to . . ." She seemed to be thinking it over. "No, I *still* believe that something's frightened Jacob, and he's blown it all out of proportion. When he's sure he can trust us, he'll talk about it. Let's don't make things worse for him by telling people the way he's acting now. He'll be embarrassed enough when it's over."

Nick could understand how she felt—her wanting to believe that Jacob was the same intelligent man he used to be and that logic would pull him through.

Nick thought of the debates they used to have at the dinner table, and how Jacob relished a good free-for-all.

"What do *you* think about that, Nick?" Jacob had asked once when they'd been discussing whether or not a reporter should have to reveal his sources. He never cared whether Nick agreed with him or not; it was how well Nick reasoned it out that mattered.

"Well," Nick had said, warming to the debate, "if newspapers can print a story about a guy without saying who told them, the guy never has a chance to face his accuser."

"But if a reporter has to make his sources public, people will be afraid to tell him anything," Mother had put in.

"Aha!" Dad had said, grinning. "It's not an open-and-shut case, is it? What do you say about that, Nick?"

Sometimes, when Nick had argued skillfully from one position, Jacob would insist that he switch sides and argue from the other, just to see if he could do it, if he were being objective.

It was hard to believe that this was the same Jacob Karpinski.

Nick walked slowly down the hall, paused at the door of his bedroom, then went on to the room at the end. Jacob was sitting in a chair by the window, chewing the nail on his middle finger. He noticed Nick in the doorway and let his hands drop.

"Dad, I didn't mean to make trouble over the box," Nick said.

Jacob Karpinski leaned forward, elbows on his knees. He was wearing the same checked shirt and khaki pants he'd worn all week. He didn't seem to notice that either. When he spoke, finally, his voice was soft. "It's not your fault, Nick. Or Wanda's either. I'm just sorry I got you into this. You have to do whatever they say. I understand."

His words seemed to scratch at the air like fingernails against a blackboard.

"Who, Dad?" Nick could barely hear himself speak. His lips stuck together and his throat was dry. "Who's 'they'? The men at the office?"

Mr. Karpinski gave a sardonic laugh. "It goes a lot deeper than that, Nick. It's a whole network."

"*What* is?" Nick walked over and sat down on the edge of the bed, close to his father's chair. "Tell me, Dad. You can trust me."

Jacob looked at him, his face drawn, eyes tired. He put one finger to his lips. "Don't let Wanda hear," he whispered.

Nick nodded. "Who are they, Dad?" he repeated.

Jacob leaned over until their shoulders touched. "The Communists," he said. "Don't tell your mother."

Three

It was as though the month of January had seeped in under the door, up the stairs and into all the open spaces of the apartment. Even when the rooms were warm, words themselves seemed covered with frost—a chill not of anger but of numbing uncertainty and disbelief.

Nick moved mechanically from class to class the next day with nothing more to hold onto except the knowledge that something was very wrong with his father.

For a few moments the previous day, he had thought it would all be made clear. He had felt, for an instant, the awful spine-tingling thrill that perhaps his father was caught up in some international intrigue—that all along Jacob Karpinski had been leading a double life, and the secret would now unfold.

"What do you mean, Dad?" he had asked, astonished. "What do the Communists want with you?"

"I know too much." Jacob seemed merely to mouth the words, his voice a hoarse whisper.

"About what?"

His father smiled slightly and turned to the window again.

"*Tell* me, Dad," Nick persisted, desperately wanting his father's trust.

"I know how they operate," Jacob said.

Nick stared at him, goose bumps rising on his arms. Jacob was talking, now. He was confiding, and in a few minutes, Nick would know. "How'd you get involved in this?" he whispered back. "You meet someone at work?"

He tried to see in Jacob's eyes the father he had always known, wishing that Dad would quit fidgeting about, just tell it to him straight.

"They're all in on it," Jacob said. "Every one of them. Even Edmunds."

Nick tried to understand. "You're *serious*? The whole Life Trust Company?"

"Shhh." Jacob put one hand on Nick's wrist. "Don't tell your mother."

Uncertainty grabbed at Nick again, dissolving

the faith he had felt only seconds before. "She's got to know, Dad."

"She won't believe me." Jacob's eyes were changing again. "No one believes me. You don't believe me yourself. You believe Edmunds."

Nick shook his head, bewildered. "Dad, I just don't know what to think."

"Listen." The fingers gripped his wrist so tightly that Nick could feel Jacob's nails digging into the flesh. "They've got spies all over. They train them there—then send them out."

"You've been with Life Trust for three years, Dad. You just find this out?"

Jacob ignored the question. "Everywhere you look, they've got spies."

"Why don't you go to the police?"

"Ha!" Jacob withdrew his hand. "The police are in on it too."

Nick's back felt cold, as though a shadow were moving across the room. "The whole Chicago police force?"

Jacob gave no answer, and the coldness settled in Nick's chest.

"Go to the FBI, then."

The smile played on Jacob's lips again. "They've infiltrated the FBI too."

When Nick spoke again, he hardly recognized his own voice. The color had gone out of the words;

his voice was flat: "What are you going to do, Dad? We going to move or what? You going to get another job?"

He watched as his father hunched over his knees again, large hands dangling, his face drawn. "Only way I'm going to leave Chicago is in a box. *They'll* see to that."

A wave of panic swept over Nick. On the outside he was the same Nick Karpinski, but he was leading a double life. They were both living double lives, he and his father.

THE TENSION seemed to build inside him the next day with each succeeding class. The casual talk and laughter in the halls were reminders of how wrong things were at home. In English, Nick seemed to have trouble breathing, as though the worry were sitting on his chest. When he got to gym, third period, he threw himself into the game with a frenzy, lurching for the volleyball out of turn, then smashing it over the net as though the ball itself were the problem. When Nick's team went to the sidelines, he stood with his leg muscles locked tightly, back rigid. Even after he had cooled off, he could not seem to slow his breathing, and suddenly he knew he was going to black out. He had the presence of mind to crouch down; the next thing he knew, he was lying flat on his back and someone was propping his feet up.

"It's okay," the coach was saying. "Just stand back. He's coming 'round."

Nick felt as though he were at the bottom of a well. He could hear their voices, but he had no energy to respond.

"Nick?" Mr. Feingold slapped him lightly on one cheek. "Can you hear me?"

Nick wanted to answer, but it was too much effort. He wondered who had hold of his feet.

There was another voice now—Fred Martin, from his English class: "One minute he was beside me and the next thing I knew he was on the floor."

Nick struggled to open his eyes.

"He's conscious. Color's coming back in his face," Feingold said. "He'll be okay. You guys go take your showers. Get going."

Sounds of retreating footsteps crossing the gym —low voices fading away.

The coach slid one hand under Nick's neck and helped him sit up. Nick felt stupid. What a dumb thing to have happened.

"You okay, now?"

"Yeah. Just got a little lightheaded there for a minute, I guess."

"You seem really hyper today, Nick. Have a fight with your girl or something?"

Nick gave a weak laugh. "No."

"Go dress and see the nurse. I want her to sign a reentry slip before you come back to class tomorrow."

"Hey, I'm fine!" Nick protested.

"See the nurse," said Feingold, and walked on down the gym toward the PE office.

It was the last thing Nick wanted. He wanted to blend in with the other students as inconspicuously as a weed in a meadow. He had wanted this all his life, in fact—to belong, to be a member of the team. He had just begun to feel at home in South Bend, just begun to break out of his shyness and make friends, when the Life Trust Company transferred his dad to Chicago. Nick had to start all over again. He'd made friends with Danny Beck and Fred Martin, however, and now there were girls in the picture, as well. Passing out in gym just wasn't on the program.

Nick shuffled off to the locker room as the bell sounded. The other boys were leaving and he had the showers to himself. He stayed under the jet of hot water for a long time; he was going to be late for the next class anyway, what did it matter? He thought of the way he had lain sprawled out on the gym floor—a huge guy like him—big ears, big feet. That sure must have been a sight. He dried off, pulled on his jeans, and headed upstairs.

Marjorie Etting, Nurse, it read on the door next to the office. Nick pushed it open and went inside.

Miss Etting looked like a young girl, but she was probably in her thirties. Some women just looked like that—as though their bodies never grew up.

She was light-haired and freckled all over, and she smiled at Nick from the file cabinet.

"Be with you in a sec," she said, noting something down on a clipboard, then came over. "How we doing?"

"I'm okay. Need a reentry form for gym tomorrow."

"Yeah?" She grinned at him. "What happened?"

"Nothing, really. Just got a little lightheaded. Guess I blacked out for a minute."

"Somebody bump into you?"

"No. I was just resting, over at the side."

She reached out and checked his pulse. "This ever happen before? Anything in your medical history that might account for it?"

"No."

"Well, let me check a couple things and then you can go. For starters, put this in your mouth."

Nick felt the thermometer slide in under his tongue. Miss Etting rolled up his sleeve and fastened a cloth band around his arm. She pulled it tight, then squeezed a rubber bulb in her hand. The band grew tighter. She released the bulb and watched a dial.

"Blood pressure's okay," she said, removing the band, then checked the thermometer. "Ditto your temperature. What'd you have for breakfast? You aren't one of those guys who goes without breakfast, are you?"

Nick shook his head. He felt awkward, childish. "Cereal," he muttered. "Toast. Look, I don't know why you're making such a fuss about this."

She laughed, "*You're* the one who's fussing, not me. Okay, I'll sign the slip, but if it happens again, in or out of school, drop by and we'll take a blood sample, check for anemia. Okay?"

"Okay."

She took the slip of paper from his hand and bent over the desk to sign it. But she did not hand it back immediately. "Sometimes," she said, "plain old garden-variety stress can do this to you. School going okay this year?"

"Sure."

"No problems at home?"

Nick felt his back stiffen. He shook his head and looked up at the clock impatiently.

"Okay. Let me give you a pass for your next class." She handed him both slips of paper. "Drop by and see me anytime. I'm here all day," she called as he went out, but Nick did not look back.

MR. CRANSTON was holding a plastic model of a cell.

"The nucleus," he said, turning the model around and pointing to a lump inside it. ". . . the nucleolus, and down here we have a vacuole. . . ."

Nick edged into the room, slipped his pass on the teacher's desk, and quickly took his seat.

"Page ninety-seven, Karpinski," Cranston said. "The section on mitosis."

Nick fumbled with the pages of his biology book, feeling the eyes of the other students on him as the teacher waited. He hunched over his textbook, embarrassed.

But as Cranston continued the lecture, Nick remembered how it had been back in Lafayette when he was in third grade, "Pinski!" "Pinski!" the boys used to chant, and it had taken him years to realize that it was as much a sign of affection as it was of teasing. If Nick reddened and fumed and glared, then "Pinski" became a taunt. If he laughed and kidded back, it drew them closer. The trouble had been with himself. Same thing here. They took their cues from him. He could sit there looking awkward and ill-at-ease—Karpinski, the creep, the jerk who fainted on the gym floor—or he could act as though coming in late was no big deal, which it wasn't. The rest of the students were probably more interested in what they were having for lunch than in Nick Karpinski and his problems. His shoulders relaxed, his breathing became easier, and he stretched one leg out into the aisle and concentrated on Cranston.

Funny about names, though.

I was named for Wanda Landowska, the famous harpsichordist, Nick's mother told him once, her narrow pointy chin tilting upward. *And you, Nick, were named for Copernicus.*

43

Copernicus was Polish? Nick had asked.

Chopin, too, and don't you forget it. The Karpinskis and the Ryceks aimed high. Mother wanted him to stand out and be recognized as much as Nick himself wanted to be anonymous. He always imagined himself in a solitary job—not because he didn't like people; he just never knew how to fit in, what to say. Now, however, he and Danny could work on it together.

Nick turned his attention to the front of the room where Mr. Cranston had set the plastic model back on the desk.

"There's a marvelous exhibit on genetics in the lobby of the Life Trust Insurance building downtown," he was saying. "If any of you happens to be down there, stop in. You can see the whole thing in twenty minutes—audio demonstrations, human embryos from conception to full term—but it's only there till March fifteenth." He smiled. "Live a little! Broaden yourselves! It's a great way to spend a Saturday. Write me a one-page report on it, and it's worth five points."

There were reminders of his father everywhere, Nick was thinking—the nurse's questions, Cranston's reference to his dad's office. . . . Even when Nick tried to forget, the problem at home seemed to ride around in his back pocket.

There was a pop quiz near the end of the period, and Nick was only halfway through, chewing on his pencil eraser, when he noticed Lois Mueller watching him from across the room. She was a short, slight girl in designer jeans and a pink sweater, and she smiled at him, then ran her hand tensely through her dark hair and stared back down at her paper. Nick smiled back, but too late for her to see it.

He was thinking again how tiny she was and forgot the quiz momentarily. They'd really be a pair going down the street together, wouldn't they? Bet she hardly came up to his shoulder. He was glad she smiled first, though. It would make things easier after class.

When the bell rang, Lois dawdled as she gathered up her books, so that Nick got over to the door about the time she was ready to leave.

"We going to try it?" she said playfully.

"What?"

"The Life Trust exhibit. Great way to spend a Saturday! Cranston said so."

Nick laughed. "We can think of something better than that. Hey, I wanted to tell you that Karen and Danny are going out with us. He called her and she said she'd go."

"Fantastic." Lois never stopped smiling. She was a smile machine, Nick was thinking, turning them out one after another. Maybe she overdid it. A guy didn't like to think that maybe a girl was laughing at him.

"How'd you do on the quiz?" he asked.

"Only got about half. Cranston must get his jollies out of springing quizzes. My brother had him six years ago and said that Cranston did the same thing back then. How did you do?"

"Not even half. I didn't read the chapter." Copernicus he was not.

They met Karen Zimmerman in the hall and walked to the cafeteria together. Karen started her nervous humming when Nick fell in step beside her, then gave it up for conversation.

"I hear we're going out with you and Lois," she said.

"Yeah. Hope there's a good movie on."

"You can always come to our apartment if there isn't," Karen offered. "Mom *loves* me to bring people home. Says it doesn't seem like Saturday night unless the place is full of people. I think she misses my sisters."

"They all move away?"

"They both got married. I'm the youngest."

Danny Beck brought his tray to their table when he saw them, and it seemed natural to Nick that the four of them should be eating together. Just like that, they were a group. It wasn't as hard as he had imagined.

They had to talk loudly to be heard above the din in the cafeteria. Nick enjoyed watching the two girls—Karen's habit of dropping her eyes when she laughed, the faces Lois made describing her brother,

46

the way the girls giggled softly at some joke between themselves.

What if this became a steady thing? What if they just started going out regularly on Saturday nights, the four of them? What if they began going around to each other's apartments, something Nick had wanted all his life—friends who felt free enough to drop in.

He was going to have to work this out—make plans, excuses, escapes. . . . It was as though some awful secret were locked away in the Karpinski apartment, and it was Nick who kept the key.

Four

SLOWLY the clinking sounds separated themselves from Nick's dream and he rolled over and looked at the clock in the darkness. A quarter past three. He raised his head from the pillow, saw the sliver of light under his door, and lay down again, trying to decipher the noise.

Mother wouldn't be cooking at this hour. He waited, felt himself slipping off into sleep, and struggled to keep his eyes open. The sounds were coming from the bathroom. Nick sat up at last and swung his legs over the side of the bed.

His feet made no noise in the hallway. The floorboards were cold. Schmidt, the super, turned the heat down to fifty-five at night, and Nick didn't usually get up unless he had to. He pulled his pajamas together at the neck and stood in the doorway of the bathroom, blinking.

Jacob Karpinski was sitting on the edge of the tub, newspapers spread out in front of him. The float for the toilet tank lay on the floor. Also the drain cover from the sink and both faucet handles. Jacob startled when he saw Nick, then went on tinkering with his screwdriver. The float fell apart at his feet.

"What are you doing?" Nick asked groggily.

Jacob glanced toward the medicine cabinet, then back to Nick. He put one finger to his lips. Nick squatted down on the floor beside him.

"What's happening?" he asked again.

"Looking for microphones."

"Microphones?" Nick stared down at the toilet float. "In there?"

"I think I know now," Jacob whispered. He stood up, pulling Nick to his feet. Opening the mirrored door of the cabinet, he pointed to the slot for used razor blades.

Nick looked at it, then at his father. If this were a movie, he could laugh. He felt like laughing anyway. Felt like treating it as some enormous joke and going back to bed. Except that he couldn't forget about it. Jokes you could forget.

"That's where it's hidden," Jacob said softly. "I know now."

The impulse to laugh turned to anger. "*How* do you know?" Nick asked, but his father didn't answer. Nick knew he wouldn't talk as long as they were there in the bathroom. He stumbled out to the couch, and Jacob followed.

"How do you know?" Nick demanded.

Jacob was only a silhouette against the hall light, and he walked as though his huge shoulders dragged him forward.

"Because I know," he said. "Everything I say is repeated back to me the next day."

"Who? Who repeats it?"

"*You* know."

"No, I don't!" Nick said. "What are you talking about?"

"Everyone," said Jacob.

Nick wearily leaned his head back over the top of the sofa and closed his eyes. He wondered sometimes if he should even listen—if that wasn't making it worse.

Jacob went on. "Remember when my brother called a couple days ago?"

"Uncle Thad? So. . . ?"

Jacob came over and crouched down beside the sofa in the half-light. "Yesterday," he whispered, "when I went down to get the mail, the first thing the postman said to me was 'brother.'"

Nick jerked his head up. "So what?"

"He said, 'Brother, the snow's never going to stop.' You know what that means, don't you? It means they're never going to let me go."

"Dad, he was just making conversation!" Nick gave a helpless laugh. "I can't *believe* this! You, of all people!"

"And then," Jacob went on, "he pointed to our box and said, 'Your mail's in the box.' And it was the way he looked at me when he said 'box.' He knows. I could tell. The only way I'm going to get out of Chicago is in a box."

Nick shivered involuntarily. His father stood up and started the restless pacing that Nick knew so well by now—over to the apartment door, then across the rug to the windows and back to the door again.

"What are you saying, Dad? That the mailman's in on it too?"

Jacob gave him a cold smile.

"You really believe that the Communists have bugged our apartment? That they're sending you messages?" Nick stared at him in disbelief. "Dad, how the heck are they getting in here?"

"They have their ways. It's not so hard when Schmidt's working for them."

Nick's voice cracked. "Now *Schmidt's* a Communist?"

"You'd be surprised."

Nick listened in despair and was surprised to find tears springing up in his eyes. "Why don't they just knock you off and get it over with?"

"That's exactly what they want to do, but they

have to torture me first. This is only the beginning." Jacob paced. "Go on to bed, Nick. You need the sleep. I'll keep an eye on things."

Nick lay staring up at the ceiling, gulping tears that ran backwards down his throat. His eyes refused to close. He heard his father tinkering in the bathroom again, then his mother's voice in the hallway. There was agitated talk between them, more footsteps, and finally Mother went back to bed.

He's crazy. The thought lodged in Nick's brain like a bullet. He had never known anyone who was mentally ill, and this was not what he expected. He expected crazy jibberish and vacant expressions, not simply a conversation that didn't quite hold together.

His mind zigzagged back and forth between the belief that his father was sick and the question of whether at least some of it was true. He settled at last on the theory that perhaps one of the men at the Life Trust Company was a Communist and had said something to Jacob. Maybe that's what it was, an overreaction, and eventually Dad would come to his senses. Nick fell asleep at last and slept through the alarm the next morning.

At ten, his mother woke him.

"Nick," she said cautiously from the doorway, "are you going to school? It's after ten."

Nick leaped out of bed, throwing off the covers.

"I just didn't know what to do—I didn't know if you'd slept . . ." his mother apologized.

Nick went down the hall to the bathroom. There were still newspapers on the floor from last night. He grabbed them up in a wad and stuffed them into the wastebasket, then showered, and went to school without breakfast.

The corridors were empty. Teachers' voices droned from classrooms, and Nick could hear the band practicing at the far end of the hall. He had already missed the first two periods, but he could sneak into gym. As he rounded the corner, however, he saw Miss Etting coming toward him.

She smiled and frowned at the same time and put out one hand to slow him down. He had no choice but to stop.

"Nick?" she said. "You okay?"

"Sure." He tried to make his voice sound light, but it betrayed him. It was still foggy.

"You look as though you hardly got any sleep."

"I was up late," he told her, moving away. "I'm all right."

He walked on down the hall, turning at the corner, then ran down the stairs to the gym. He was going to have to be more careful. His eyes would give him away.

IT SNOWED again on Saturday. The boys had planned to take their dates to a theater over on Lincoln Avenue, but at noon the snow had already reached four inches and was still coming down.

Danny called at two.

"Just our luck," he said. "You think we should take them to the movie on Broadway instead?"

"What's playing there?"

"The Blood Suckers."

"Cripes!" said Nick. "We don't want to take them there—not on the first date."

"We could just fool around in the snow, then."

Nick's voice broke with exasperation. "Danny, we promised them a movie. We can't just fool around in the snow instead."

"Oh." Danny sighed. "Well, let's wait a while longer and see what happens."

The snow stopped about five and Danny called again. "Let's try for the theater on Lincoln. Wear boots," he said. "I'll go ahead and pick up Karen, and then we'll come by for you."

"No, I'll be waiting in the lobby," Nick said quickly. "I'll meet you there."

Nick showered, put on his best cords and a gray sweater.

"Going out, Nick?" his mother asked at dinner, setting a stew on the table.

"Yeah. Danny and I are taking some girls to the movies."

His mother's face lit up, and she glanced at her husband, but Jacob showed no expression at all. He was cracking peanuts from a bowl on a side table. Nick concentrated on the stew.

54

Mrs. Karpinski passed him the bread. "Who's the girl?"

"Lois Mueller. Danny's taking Karen."

"That girl who lives on the other side of our building? How nice!" Mother said.

The peanut shells kept piling up beside Jacob's plate and he chewed loudly, mechanically, eyes on the opposite wall.

Nick was downstairs by seven. He went out back to test the depth of the snow, lifing his feet one at a time. About eight inches, he guessed. He saw Danny come in the front entrance and go up the left stairway to Karen's apartment. Five minutes later they were down again and Nick came in from the park, stamping his feet.

"Don't you love it?" Karen said when she saw him.

"We'll have the streets to ourselves," Nick told her.

When they picked up Lois, she was wearing a down jacket, velvet pants, and suede boots that were laced up to the knees. Her neck was swathed in layers of pink and purple scarves, and she looked like something that should be standing in the window of Marshall Fields, Nick thought. Pretty, though.

It turned out to be a great evening, the kind of occasion that worked out even better than you had planned. There were only six other people in the theater. The movie was a love comedy, and every time the couple kissed, Nick and his friends sighed loudly, supplying the sound effects. No one seemed to mind.

Going back home down the middle of the street, they sang, arms around each other to keep their balance, slipping and sliding on the snow. Nick had never felt this good in his entire life.

The deli was closed, so they went to the Golden Buddha and ordered fried wontons and tea.

"Tonight was so much fun!" said Karen.

Nick and Danny beamed at her.

"If I haven't ruined my boots," said Lois. "I'm not supposed to get them wet."

Somehow that struck them all as funny, and they broke into laughter. It was snowing again, and they were the only customers in the restaurant, so the waiter brought another pot of tea and a saucer of fortune cookies.

"He who talks without thinking says nothing," Danny read aloud. He wadded it up. "I don't like the ones that preach at you," he said.

Nick bit open his cookie and extracted the narrow slip of white paper. "A distant place beckons," he read.

"Now that's more like it," Danny told him. "I'll trade."

The girls were laughing together over Karen's fortune. Danny took it away from her and read it aloud: "Be sure of your friends," he said. Lois looked at Karen and they giggled again.

"What's so funny?" Nick wanted to know.

Karen struggled to be serious. "You never know about friends, that's all."

"*Sometimes*," said Lois, "people don't even give their right names when they call you up."

Nick slid down in his seat, grinning, eyes on his hands, embarrassed. Danny was doing the same and their knees touched under the table. The girls laughed aloud together, and then Nick and Danny joined in.

"Okay," Nick said. "How'd you know?"

"Lois called me just before you did and warned me," Karen told him.

Danny looked at Lois. "How did *you* know?"

"Your voice, Danny!" She tried to imitate it. "'Of *course* I'm Nick Karpinski!' It was a scream!"

Nick and Danny smiled ruefully at each other.

"Well, it worked, didn't it?" Danny said finally.

Karen smiled at them both. "Yeah, but don't try it again. Okay?"

They walked home slowly, the boys with their arms around the girls. It was easy enough saying goodnight to Lois because the others were there. When they reached the building where Nick and Karen lived, however, things suddenly seemed awkward. They stood outside the entrance talking, and Nick didn't know whether he should go in or not. Once he put his hand on the door latch, but Danny gave him such a pleading look that he backed off.

"Well . . ." Karen said finally, digging the toe of her boot in the snow.

Danny laughed self-consciously. "Well . . ." he mimicked.

Nick fidgeted over by the door, trying to signal Danny to wind things up, to say goodnight. Instead, Danny made a snowball and aimed at a passing truck. He missed. He made another and aimed at a tree. Missed that too. Nick and Karen laughed.

"Hey, Danny!" Nick kidded. "What's this about you wanting to pitch for the White Sox?"

Danny threw a snowball at Nick next.

"Careful! The window!" Nick laughed, positioning himself against the glass.

At that moment Karen reached down to dig some ice out of her boot, and Danny slipped the next snowball down her back. Nick watched in horror as Karen rose up with a shriek, wriggling about. The grin on Danny's face faded fast.

"I'm . . . I'm sorry!" Danny gasped.

Karen shrieked again, flailing her arms, her body twisting as the snowball made its slow descent. Nick and Danny stood frozen to the sidewalk.

Some girls would have gone inside in a huff, Nick thought. Lois, probably, would have slammed the door. But Karen managed to salvage the evening.

"Well," she said finally, taking off her coat and shaking out the last bit of snow, "that's what I get for not going right in. Goodnight, guys. Thanks for the movie, Danny."

"Honestly," Danny spluttered. "I didn't mean . . . I didn't think . . . !"

"Goodnight." She laughed. "Let's do it again, sometime. Without the snowball." And she was gone.

Danny leaned against the brick, eyes closed. "Why did I do it, Nick?" he asked miserably.

"I don't know," Nick told him.

"She hates me."

"She does not. She wouldn't have said she wanted to go out again."

"I'm a jerk! I really wanted to kiss her!"

Nick laughed out loud. "She probably would have put a snowball down *you*. She'll go out with you again, Danny. You'll see."

Reassured at last, Danny started for home and Nick went inside. Smiling. Despite the fiasco about Karen's fortune and the snowball down her back, the evening had gone okay. Nick realized that all his life he had wondered what it would feel like to be part of a group such as this. It felt good.

IN FEBRUARY, Jacob Karpinski got a new job. He had gone out one morning, taken a civil service entrance exam, and was hired two weeks later as a temporary mail sorter at a branch post office.

"You know, I really think the worst is over," Mother said that evening before dinner. "Thank goodness. We've been living off savings the last few weeks. Now Jacob's getting a regular paycheck again."

Her words were like a cool, long-awaited breeze to Nick. Relief seeped from every pore. He should have had more faith, should have known the craziness was just too ridiculous to continue.

"A *government* job," Mother went on. "Just what Jacob said he wanted. He'll feel more secure, I think, and that will make a big difference. He'll work his way up to management in no time."

Nick's father rose early in the mornings and was off before Nick took his shower. He got home around four and spent all his time at the desk in the bedroom until the music students were gone. There were maps to study, diagrams, charts, booklets. . . .

"He has to learn every street in his zip code!" Wanda Karpinski said in a telephone call to her parents one Saturday while Jacob was at work. "If they make him a career appointment, it will be a secure job, Papa, with pension and health benefits. Maybe it was all for the best. There was so much pressure on him at Life Trust. A man can take only so much. . . ."

Nick tried hard to keep out of his father's way in the days that followed. In the evenings he listened as Jacob recited the lists of streets, avenues, courts, drives, roads, boulevards—Mother correcting when he made a mistake. Jacob was working now, he was studying, and if he was still silent at the dinner table, it was because he had so much to learn in so short a time. They all understood that.

Sometimes, however, in spite of Dad's new job, Mother seemed edgy herself, easily offended. Once, when she made a cheerful remark and Nick did not immediately respond, she turned on him suddenly, vehemently, seemingly without reason:

"*Don't* talk, then," she snapped.

And Nick, hurt and confused, sat stunned, unable to answer.

But most days were not like that. Most of the time it was Nick and his mother quizzing Dad after dinner on a new list of streets, and if Jacob did not smile much, it was because the last few months had been so unsettling; he needed time to sort things out. Nick concentrated on his own studies and his grades improved. Mother seemed happier. They were a family again, just like the Becks and the Zimmermans.

One Tuesday Grandma Rycek took the train in from Hammond and spent the whole day with Mother. When Nick got home from school, the kitchen was full of her baking. There was even a platter of small fried doughnuts on the coffee table for the music students, since lessons had already begun.

"Wow. You've been busy," Nick smiled at her, and Grandma reached out and hugged him.

"When I'm happy, I bake," she said, "and I am happy that things are going better here." She motioned toward a pan of veal and dumplings on the stove. "For your father," she said. "You tell him I'm happy for him, for his new job."

She left to take the el back downtown, then the train to Hammond, and the sounds of a piano duet came from the study.

Nick did his homework in his room and turned his radio on low, his foot keeping time with the beat. At five-thirty he came out to set the table for dinner. Mother was giving her last lesson in the study. Nick frowned to himself. His father should have been home.

At six, the student left and Mother came out to the kitchen.

"Jacob's not here?" she said.

"Guess not."

She went to the window in the living room and peered down at the street below.

"Mama made veal paprika especially for him," she said, as if to herself.

"Maybe they kept him overtime," Nick offered. "He said there would be overtime once in a while."

"That's probably it. We'll wait a little."

Nick went back in his room and listened to the radio, but his eye kept drifting toward the clock.

"We should eat," his mother said finally from the doorway. "The dumplings won't be good if we don't. We'll keep some warm for Jacob."

All through dinner, Mother chattered on, but her words came too fast, her voice too tight, too high. Food slipped down Nick's throat but he couldn't taste it. Finally, worn out by her own talking, Mother fell silent and toyed with the piece of meat on her plate.

"I'm going out back and see if his car's there," Nick said suddenly. "He usually tries to find a space in the park."

"Yes, you look for him, Nick, and I'll stay here by the phone in case he calls."

Nick went downstairs and out the rear entrance to the oval-shaped park. Every space around its perimeter was filled with cars, bumper to bumper. By eight, the only parking spaces left were blocks away.

In summer Jacob usually tried to park beside the cluster of evergreens down at one end, Nick knew. In winter, he opted for as close as he could get to the door. Nick looked up and down the drive for the blue Pontiac, but in the dim light of the streetlamps, all cars looked the same color, a blackish gray.

He walked around the west end and started down the other side, conscious of a car motor idling, and realized he had been hearing the sound ever since he came out—as though someone were warming up a car, but never drove off. There was something familiar about the noise—the sound of the Pontiac, maybe, and he quickened his steps. The motor grew louder, and Nick began to search out the blue top in the darkness.

The Pontiac had been parked on the circular drive at the east end, away from the streetlights. From the sound of the motor, it had been running a long time. Nick broke into a run and stooped down at the window. It was his father's car, but the driver's seat was empty. Nick looked around, then opened the car door and turned off the ignition. The key dangled in the lock.

Nick crawled inside and looked over the seat. Empty. He got out. "Dad?" he called. There was no answer.

He took the keys and locked the door, then started around the car. He had just reached the trunk when he stumbled over something there in the snow, and then he heard his father moan.

Nick whirled around, skidding on the ice, and grabbed hold of his father's shoulders. "Dad!" he said again, his heart in his mouth.

His father began to cough. One big hand reached out and pushed Nick roughly away.

"You must have fallen!" Nick said, trying to figure it out. Then he saw his father's coat wadded up and placed like a pillow on the snow, just beneath the exhaust pipe.

Five

THE LEFT WALL in Miss Etting's office was covered with posters. *Think!* said one, showing a girl looking down at a pack of cigarettes in her hand. *It's the only bod you've got.* Another showed a group of runners from the waist up, faces intent, muscles taut: *Protein, carbohydrates, vitamins, and minerals,* it said underneath.

Outside in the hall, students were milling about, shouting and joking on their way back from the cafeteria. The nurse closed the transom over her door to shut out the noise, then sat down across from Nick.

"What's up?" she said cheerfully. Her eyes never left his face.

Nick gave a little smile. "I've got this friend . . ." he said, and swallowed. "He keeps telling me these stories, and I'm sort of worried about him."

"What sort of stories?"

"It's his father. I mean, it's really weird."

"Tell me."

Nick shrugged and shifted slightly in his chair. "Well, a few months ago, around Christmas, I guess, he . . . the father, I mean . . . started acting like somebody was after him. This friend—I can't tell you his name—finally got his dad to talk about it, and the father insists that the Communists are trying to kill him. That his whole company is Communist. So he just walked off the job."

Miss Etting studied him intently.

"My friend's really worried," Nick went on. "Last night, his father lay down by the exhaust pipe of his car and left the motor running. He . . . my friend . . . doesn't know what to do. I don't know what to tell him."

"It sounds like something worth worrying about," the nurse said at last. She drew her legs up on the chair and tucked her feet beneath her. "What puzzles me is why your friend thinks it's *his* problem. Isn't there a mother in the picture?"

"She doesn't want anyone else to know about it. She'd really be mad if she knew he'd told me."

"No older brothers? Sisters? No relatives?"

"There aren't any brothers or sisters," Nick answered. "I just wondered, I mean, it sounds so bizarre, but is it possible that there *could* be a whole company that's a Communist front here in Chicago? That he's telling the truth?"

"What do you think, Nick?"

"Sounds a little far out."

"*Anything* is possible. But not probable."

They sat for a moment without talking, then Nick said, "I guess my friend's sort of worried that his dad is . . . you know . . . cracking up. He says now he's talking about the apartment super being a Communist. I mean, I've seen his father, and anybody looking at the man would think he was normal, that's what's so strange."

"Nick, this is a problem that's a lot bigger than you and me and your friend," Miss Etting told him. "I think that the man is very sick and needs help. Somebody's got to convince the mother."

Hearing those words said aloud, Nick didn't know what it was he felt—relief or fear. However terrifying it would be to have the Communists after his father—after him, even—the danger would be out there somewhere—outside themselves. But the thought of his father mentally ill was even more frightening. It was like living with a traitor in the family, because the danger came from within.

He realized he hadn't talked for several minutes and stared down at his hands, which seemed detached from his arms, dangling strangely off the ends of the arm rests.

"Well," he said finally, "that's what I sort of figured too. I just wanted to know what you thought about it."

Miss Etting leaned forward. "I hope that someone —a relative, maybe—is able to get through to the mother, because obviously the man is a danger to himself. And he *could* be—I'm not saying that he is —but he could be a danger to others as well."

Nick got up, his chest suddenly tight. "Well, I'll tell my friend that," he said. "Thanks a lot."

Miss Etting followed him to the door. "Listen, Nick, if this friend wants to talk with me, please give him my number." She took a card from her pocket and scribbled something on the back. "I don't usually give this out, but that's my home phone. He can call me anytime. You tell him that."

"Thanks," Nick said again. He pulled out his wallet and stuck the card behind his student ID. Then he went out into the hall, heart pounding.

There were twenty minutes left of the lunch period. Someone had given the problem a name now. It was an illness, and as though a hand were pushing him from behind, Nick felt himself propelled forward and he moved quickly, before he lost his nerve. Right now, Uncle Thad was at lunch. Didn't he usually have just a sandwich in his office? Wouldn't this be the best time to call? Maybe he'd gone out, though. Maybe the receptionist would answer and tell Uncle Thad later that Nick had called, and then Thad would call home and Dad would wonder. . . .

No, if he was going to do it, Nick thought, he had to do it now, before he changed his mind. He remembered the public phone in the basement near the gym. There usually wasn't anyone around at this hour. He veered left and passed the band room where Danny was playing the drums.

"Hey, Nick!" called Danny.

"Can't stop!" Nick yelled back, and sped on around the corner. Far down the corridor he saw Karen and Lois walking slowly toward him, eating apples. He ducked in the library, lost himself in the maze of bookshelves, then exited out the door on the other side and on down the stairs to ground level.

He fished for change in his pocket and inserted the coins. One ring, two. Then: "Personalized Products, may I help you?"

"Hello, is Thaddeus Karpinski there, please?"

"May I tell him who's calling?"

"It's private."

There was a pause. "I'll see if he's in. He may be out to lunch."

There was a wait so long that Nick's palms began to sweat; student voices came nearer, then receded, and Nick expected that at any moment the gym door would open and some of the guys would come over and try to listen in.

Then it was Uncle Thaddeus on the other end. "Hello?"

"This is Nick."

"Nick! Well, for heaven sake! Shirley said I had a mystery caller. Couldn't imagine—"

"Uncle Thad, I'm calling from school; I didn't want to call from home. Do you have a couple minutes? It's my lunch period."

"Sure. What's the matter?"

"It's serious. It's about Dad."

There was a pause. "What about him?"

"He's sick. There's something wrong. I think he's mentally ill."

Why did the silence on the other end make him suspect that Uncle Thad already knew?

"What makes you think that?" his uncle said at last.

"He walked out on his job at Life Trust."

"When?"

"Weeks ago."

"I'm surprised, but that hardly makes him mentally ill."

"Uncle Thad, last night he tried to kill himself."

"What? Nick, I saw him at Thanksgiving. He looked fine!"

"Well, he's not fine now. Something's wrong." Nick explained what had happened.

Again the long, uneasy silence. Finally, "Where is he?"

"Home, I suppose."

"I'll call."

"No. Please. He'd be furious if he knew I called you. Can't you just come by?"

"Well, I guess. Maybe this weekend."

"Thanks. Please don't tell Mom, either."

Nick sat through history scarcely hearing. He felt limp, tired beyond all reason. At last he had managed to pass the responsibility onto someone else. He had opened the door to the secret just a little and admitted Uncle Thad. But Thad was Jacob's brother; why *shouldn't* he be told?

The teacher was talking about the Franco-Prussian war, but Nick was reliving the night before when he had found his father in the snow. Mother simply had not believed him.

"He *must* have fallen, Nick," she'd said, as they helped Jacob into a chair.

"Mom, he had his coat rolled up under his head, and he was lying there by the tail pipe!"

"My God! My God!" she kept saying as she rushed about the kitchen, heating up the coffee, wrapping blankets around Jacob, who looked groggy and sick there at the table.

That morning, however, Mrs. Karpinski had said, "He's so sorry, Nick. He told me. I'm sure he'll never try something like that again. He said he got a poor rating at the post office and was terribly upset."

"So upset he'd try to kill himself?"

They each sat without speaking for a few minutes, mulling it over.

"It wasn't a really serious attempt, was it?" Mother said finally. "He must have known it wouldn't work; he knew he'd be found!"

"I just don't know, Mom." Nick picked up his toast, then put it down again. "How could he get a poor rating? He's been an insurance underwriter! He's got a college education! How come he can't sort mail?"

"I think it's just the change. He can't concentrate. He told me so himself. He cried, Nick—he's just so sorry he caused us all that worry." Wanda Karpinski had pressed her lips together. "It's the first time . . . I've ever seen him really cry. Once he adjusts to this job, his rating will improve. You'll see."

Nick was getting his coat from his locker after school when Karen and Lois finally caught up with him.

"Where have you been hiding all day?" Lois teased. "Didn't see you in the cafeteria at all."

Nick managed a smile. "Had some work to make up."

"Well, come on, we're meeting Danny by the west door and going for a hamburger."

Nick sat in a booth at Jimmy's Sub Shop carrying on a conversation with his friends and another with himself, both at the same time. While his face was smiling, he was asking himself questions he could not answer. Until last December, his father had seemed normal, hadn't he? Even Uncle Thad said so. What was it that had set him off—had stretched his nerves to the breaking point?

Nick thought of all the times his father had knocked on the door of his room asking him to turn down his stereo. The way Nick always left his sneakers in the hallway for someone to trip over; his habit of leaving a glass right on the edge of the table for someone to knock off. Obviously, he wasn't the type of son who was easy to live with, who was easy on the nerves. And what about when he was small, and every time they went someplace he whined? He didn't remember whining. He remembered only asking for a White Sox baseball cap or an ice cream cone or begging to stop for some gum, but his father had called it whining, so it must have been.

"Nick, you are a thousand miles away."

It was Karen's voice. The worries were getting through.

"Sorry," he said, and even forced a whistle as they left the shop.

As he went up the stairs later to the apartment, he tried to think how to tell Mother what Miss Etting had said without letting her know he had talked with the nurse. As it turned out, he didn't have to. As Mother was setting the table for dinner, her back to Nick, she said, "I called a mental health clinic this morning. I didn't give them our name or anything, but I just thought maybe we should have some advice about how to handle things . . . till Jacob's better."

Her voice had become so soft Nick had to strain to hear, as though she didn't want him to hear, didn't even want to say the words herself.

"What did they tell you?" he asked.

"They think he should be in a hospital. I *told* them he's working and everything . . . it's not as though he's raving."

"He's mentally ill, Mom. You know that."

She winced. "He's mentally *disturbed*, Nick. There's a difference. I told them we're going to solve this outside a hospital. Jacob would do the same for me. I refuse to humiliate him."

"What if he gets worse?"

"Well, what if he gets better?" Her voice took on a sudden sharpness. "*I'm* going to be optimistic about this, Nick. You can go looking for trouble if you want, but I'm going to expect improvement. If we don't have any confidence in Jacob, he'll lose confidence in himself."

Maybe she was right, Nick thought. If *he* was sick, wouldn't he rather be at home than in a hospital? Wouldn't he want his parents to do everything they could first?

THADDEUS KARPINSKI was not as large a man as Jacob, but he had the same big ears, same

74

hairline. He arrived on Sunday afternoon about three and took the family by surprise, all but Nick.

"Thad, why didn't you let us know you were coming and I would have saved lunch for you," Mother told him. "You can stay for dinner?"

Uncle Thad kissed her, shook hands with Jacob and Nick. His face did not give away Nick's phone call, and again Nick felt relief. Now Uncle Thad would see. He was several years older than Jacob, and he would know what to do.

Nick sat down in the living room beside his uncle while Mother brought out some sliced ham, with rolls and coffee.

Jacob sat stiffly across the room in the brown chair, elbows pointing out at an angle to his body, mouth stretched into a tight smile.

"I was just in the neighborhood and thought I'd drop by," Uncle Thad said.

Jacob continued to smile. "You were just in the neighborhood, all the way from Downers Grove, on a Sunday?"

"Had a delivery to make; the man wasn't home yesterday," Thad said, and obediently laid a slice of ham across a buttered roll and took a nibble off one end.

Mrs. Karpinski pushed the platter just a little closer to him on the coffee table. "How is the stationery business going, Thad?"

75

"I'm making Sunday deliveries, so can't complain," said Thaddeus, and smiled back at her. "How are things with you, Jacob?"

Jacob's smile stretched even tighter. "You didn't hear?"

Nick could tell the way his uncle rubbed his thumb and forefinger together that he was debating what to say. "What's there to hear?" he asked finally.

Mrs. Karpinski looked cautiously at her husband, and finally, when he didn't answer, answered for him: "He's not working at Life Trust anymore, Thad."

"No? Why not?"

Nick watched his uncle put more sugar in his coffee. The room had gone very quiet. Embarrassingly quiet. Mother sat with her eyes on her lap, waiting for Jacob to answer.

"It was time to leave, that's all," Jacob said.

The silence went on. Uncle Thad took a drink of coffee, then a bite of roll, and continued chewing. Nick felt his heart sink. This is all there would be to it. Uncle Thad would finish his lunch and go home. But then he heard his uncle say,

"Jacob, how's your health? You don't look as though you've been sleeping so well. Not a health problem, is there?"

Everyone seemed to be waiting.

"It was a mistake to come here—to leave South Bend."

"Why's that?" asked Thad. "I thought you were pleased with the transfer."

"It was a mistake," Jacob said again, and sat close-mouthed, his smile gone.

"Well, what are you going to do, then? You have another job lined up?"

"He's working at the post office now," Mrs. Karpinski put in quickly.

"The post office? Well!" Uncle Thaddeus looked relieved and extended his smile to Nick. "That's a secure job, Jacob. The government may not pay the best, but there are a lot of benefits. What are you doing there?"

"Would you believe?" said Jacob. "Sorting mail."

Uncle Thad looked surprised. "Well, it's certainly something different," he said.

Nick despaired at how easily the conversation drifted away from what was important to what was not. After a few more remarks about the training period, they were talking about Thad's stationery business again.

Uncle Thad stayed for about an hour. When he got up to leave, Nick said, "I'm going over to Danny's for a while—I'll walk down with you."

He ignored the caution in his mother's eyes, put on his jacket, and stood at the door waiting for the goodbye handshake all around.

This time, however, Thad put one hand on Jacob's shoulder. "Looks like you could use about a month's vacation," he said. "Sure everything's all right, Jacob?"

"*I'm* all right," Jacob said sardonically.

"Well, let me hear from you occasionally." Thad turned to Mother. "You call me if he won't, Wanda."

"Of course," said Mother, kissing him on the cheek.

Nick and his uncle went downstairs without saying anything. It wasn't until they reached the lobby that Nick turned to him earnestly.

"Uncle Thad, you didn't *see*! You didn't see the worst at all."

"You know what I think, Nick?" His uncle held open the glass door with one large hand and waited until Nick had gone out. Then Nick opened the next door and held it for his uncle. "I think he's going through some kind of mid-life crisis. Happens to people occasionally. They make a career of one job and suddenly find out it's not what they wanted to do at all. It's pretty upsetting, starting over in your forties. Once your dad settles in on the new job, he'll feel better."

"He tried to *kill* himself, Uncle Thad."

Thaddeus walked on without answering as though he didn't want to think about it. Nick grabbed his arm with a ferocity that surprised even himself.

"Don't you even care?"

This time Uncle Thad stopped walking and looked at Nick with puzzled concentration. "Nick, why didn't your mother tell me that if it happened? Why didn't she call that night?"

"You don't even believe it happened?" Nick said incredulously.

"I'm asking you. Why didn't she call me?"

"Because she's embarrassed to have you know. She doesn't want anyone to know! She keeps saying he's going to be all right."

"Well, then, she must feel that he is and that this is something she can handle." Uncle Thad put one arm around Nick's shoulder and they walked on a little further. "Maybe you're seeing more in this than is really there."

"He's your *brother*," Nick said in desperation.

Uncle Thad's arm dropped again just as suddenly. "Look, Nick. I don't interfere when I'm not asked. Jacob leads his life, I lead mine. Your mother is in a much better position to make a judgment than I am. And if she needs me, all she has to do is call. Okay?"

Nick stood there on the sidewalk as his uncle drove away. A chill seemed to seep up through the concrete and through his legs. *He leads his life, I lead mine.* What cold words. Had Uncle Thad always been this way? Was the Karpinski side of the family always so distant and aloof, so different from the Ryceks, and Nick had never noticed?

He walked on over to Danny's apartment building, shoulders hunched, hands thrust tightly down into the pockets of his jeans. He tried to put together pieces of what he knew about his father's people, but there weren't that many pieces to work with. Both Jacob's parents were dead, and Nick had never known them. Holidays in the past had always been spent with his mother's side of the family, relatives coming in and out, talking and laughing and sharing their lives. Thinking back on those holidays now, it had always seemed that Jacob was more like an observer. Not that the Ryceks didn't try to make him feel welcome, didn't include him in their plans. Jacob never extended himself, never seemed, in fact, to know how.

When Nick got to Danny's, he found that his friend wasn't home. He went back to the deli, bought a slice of cheesecake, ate it in front of his apartment building, and then went back upstairs. When he walked in, he found himself in the middle of an argument between his parents, but it wasn't about Thad. Nick went on to his room, leaving his door open, however, so that he could listen:

"When did it come?" His father's voice—cold, suspicious.

"Yesterday, Jacob! What does it matter?"

"Why didn't you tell me?"

"So I'm telling you! It was lying right here by the lamp. You could have read it yourself." There was anger in his mother's voice, but then Nick heard her suddenly say in desperation—pleading, almost:

"It's just a buffet dinner, Jacob! You've *met* the Olsons! I've been teaching Kathleen for two years. Can't we ever go out and have a normal life like everyone else? Can't we even get a dinner invitation without all these suspicions?"

"Well, go if you want to."

"I will, Jacob, but we're both invited."

"They have it all planned, don't they? They'll get me over there, away from the apartment, and the Commies will make their move."

"*Who* has it planned? The *Olsons*?"

"*You* know."

"Stop it!" Mother screamed, and Nick's body seemed to freeze at the sound, every hair on his arms standing upright, frozen rigid. He had never heard his mother shriek that way.

"It's like a disease, Jacob." Mother was sobbing now. "First it was the people at Life Trust. Then Mr. Schmidt! Now it's the Olsons! When will you start suspecting Thad or Nick or me?"

Nick could hear soft footsteps, his father's footsteps, and he envisioned his father going to her, putting his arms around her as he had in the past when she was upset about something. But this time the footsteps didn't stop; they turned into the familiar pacing that had become a household rhythm now— a rhythm broken each time his father reached a rug, back and forth beside the windows, to the door, then the windows once again. . . .

And then his father's voice, as cold as though a door had opened and a wind were rushing through, stopping the clocks:

"Don't let him kid you, Wanda; Thad knows a lot more than he's telling."

Six

ON THE THIRD of March, a Friday, Lois called.

"It's for you, Nick, a girl!" His mother smiled, holding one hand over the mouthpiece.

Nick was embarrassed. It was the first time a girl had ever called him. Jacob watched silently from his end of the table.

"Hello?"

"Nick, did I catch you at a bad time?"

"No, I was just sitting around." Nick turned away from the table and leaned against the wall. His mother immediately took the hint and began clearing off the supper dishes, but Jacob sat unmoving, and Nick could almost feel his father's eyes burning into the back of his head.

"Karen and I just had this great idea!" Lois went on. "The yearbook is selling spaces for personal pictures—you know, your own group of friends and stuff. It's supposed to be a good day tomorrow. Why don't the four of us go out, take some pictures, and buy a space in the yearbook? I don't think it costs much."

Nick laughed. "Okay. Want me to bring the camera?"

"Great. I'll call Danny. If it's okay with him, we'll be by for you around one."

"No, we'll pick you up," Nick said hastily.

"Who was that?" Jacob said, his fingers resting tensely on the edge of the table.

"A girl." Nick started to leave the kitchen, but Jacob grabbed his arm.

"Who?"

Nick angrily wrestled his arm away. "Lois Mueller. That okay? That okay with you?"

"Let him be, Jacob. Be glad he has some friends," said Nick's mother, and Nick went quickly on into his room.

He didn't much like being home anymore—was glad for any excuse to get out. He alternated between wanting to escape and wanting to know every minute what was happening back at the apartment. Nick was learning to take pleasure in the moment—the taste of ice cream, the feel of a soft breeze, the sounds of his record collection—these were all pleasures that he could enjoy. Along with this sporadic enjoyment, however, came an undertow of guilt. How could he find amusement in anything when Dad was so sick, when Mom was so worried? How selfish could he be?

Saturday, as Lois had predicted, was sunny. The wind had lost its sharpness and the sun felt warmer on their heads. Nick met Danny and Karen in the lobby and together they went for Lois. Each of them had arranged to wear a different sort of cap. Nick had on a Greek fisherman's cap, Lois wore her brother's sailor hat, Danny had on a baseball cap, and Karen, most ingenious of all, was wearing an ancient hat of her mother's with feathers and flowers all over the top.

They walked down Diversey toward the lake and through the high-ceilinged tunnel that led from the boat launch and moorings out to the lake. The water was rough inside the tunnel, sloshing up onto the walkway beside the graffiti-covered walls. When they emerged on the other side, they ran up the rocky steps where men in old jackets fished for smelt that ran in the spring. The fishermen eyed the foursome with dry good humor and one was persuaded to take pictures of them all together on the top step, silhouetted against the sky. They stood with arms around each other, hair blowing, each holding the other's cap on for good measure. Then they changed hats for the next picture, and Danny clowned around in the hat with feathers. It was like another world here by the water, light years away from the apartment.

"As soon as you've got the pictures developed, let us see them," Lois told Nick as he turned the lever on his camera.

The day was still young, the air balmy, and nobody, least of all Nick, wanted to go home.

"I've got it!" Lois said merrily as they walked back beside the gun club and driving range. "Let's take the el and go downtown."

"What for?" Danny asked.

"It's a project Nick and I have to do. You might as well come along."

Nick was laughing now. "What?"

"The genetics exhibit in the Life Trust building, remember? Cranston said he'd give us an extra five points if we saw the exhibit and wrote a one-page report."

"No way," Danny told her.

"Oh, come on! You'll *love* it! Cranston said so, didn't he, Nick? 'A great way to spend a Saturday.'"

Karen was giggling. "Let's go."

Nick did not care to be reminded of where his father once worked, but he smiled and walked back up toward Diversey with them to the el.

IT WAS ABOUT a twenty-minute ride to State Street and a five-minute walk from there to the Life Trust Building. A guard sitting at a desk inside the door pointed their way toward the exhibit in the lobby.

Along the walls, colorful charts showed many of the things Nick had learned in class—Mendel's experiments with red and white-flowered pea plants, the structure of DNA, mutations, natural selection, and the contribution of Charles Darwin. There were electronic displays, with buttons to press, and little alcoves where short filmstrips showed continuously. At one end of the room, a scientist was demonstrating how students could perform their own experiments on fruit flies, and a small group of teenagers was watching as he prepared his culture.

Somewhere in this building, Nick was thinking, it had all begun with his father, the suspicions, the fear—a private mutation. He came to a chart titled "Hereditary Diseases," and the chart had divided them into two groups—those which were inherited directly, such as hemophilia and Huntington's Chorea, and those for which only a tendency to develop the disease was inherited: cancer, diabetes, tuberculosis, insanity, and allergies, the chart said. The pounding in Nick's chest seemed to travel up his throat and vibrate inside his head.

Lois went back to the guard and asked if he had any paper and pencils they could borrow. He tore off a couple of his unused sign-in sheets and gave her some pencils with *Maywood Park Race Track* printed on the side.

The four friends milled about the lobby, sometimes together, sometimes apart. When he had finished the mutations section, Nick sat down to make notes, and had just scribbled out one paragraph when he saw a stocky man in a dark suit come out of the elevator and walk up to the desk.

"I called a cab, Mr. Connelly," the guard said, "but it'll be a few minutes. The Shriners are marching today—there's a traffic tie-up."

"That's okay, Jim. I'll just wait over by the door," the man replied. "Nice day out there. Looks like spring is just around the corner."

"Yes, sir. Indeed it does."

Nick's heart skipped a beat. He had thought the man looked familiar somehow. Nick had seen him once at a company picnic. He would never get another chance like this one. Looking back over his shoulder, he saw that Danny and the girls were watching a filmstrip. He got up and walked quickly over to the door where Mr. Connelly had set down his briefcase and was cleaning his glasses with a pocket handkerchief.

"Mr. Connelly?"

The man turned, looked at Nick, then put on his glasses again. "Yes?"

"I'm Nick Karpinski, Jacob's son. Could I talk with you for just a minute?"

Mr. Connelly's face showed a flicker of recognition. "Why, certainly."

"My dad. . . ." Nick swallowed. "I just wondered if you knew what it was that upset him enough to quit."

"Well, you know, Nick, if you hadn't asked me that, I would have put the same question to you. How is he? Where's he working now?"

"He's got a job with the post office."

"The post office? Doing what?"

"Sorting mail. I just . . . thought maybe something had happened here that really upset him, and that maybe you knew."

"I wish I could help. I really do. Your father was an excellent underwriter, but he was never an easy man to get close to, Nick. That's not a criticism—it's just the way he was." The man paused. "He was passed by for a promotion last fall—I don't know if you knew that. Maybe that bothered him more than we thought. He seemed to be keeping to himself quite a bit, and then one day he just walked out."

A cab pulled up in front and the driver leaned over, looking through the glass doors. Mr. Connelly signaled the driver to wait, then turned again to Nick. "I'm not a doctor," he said, picking up his briefcase, "but I think your dad needs some expert help. If he's working for the government now, that's good, because they have some very fine health plans. You tell him I wish him the very best. Tell him that for me."

Nick nodded.

Mr. Connelly walked outside and got in the cab, and when Nick turned, he saw Danny and the girls watching him from the exhibit hall.

"Who was that?" Danny asked.

"Some guy my dad knew once," Nick said, stuffing his notes in his jacket pocket. "Anybody interested in some Mexican food over on Clark Street? I've seen enough genetics for one day."

"Hey! All right!" said Danny. "Let's go."

EACH TIME Nick went home, he secretly hoped that the apartment would be empty—that he would find a note from his mother saying that Jacob had entered a hospital—that someone had taken charge. When he came back from downtown, however, nothing had changed. Mother was putting away the sheet music from her Saturday classes and Jacob was standing at the window in the living room, staring down, as usual, at the street. He turned as Nick came in.

"Hi," Nick said, and went on back to his room. He took off his cap and put it on the desk beside his camera and notes from the exhibit.

"Where did you get a cap like that?" his father asked from the doorway.

Nick shut his eyes for a moment, facing the wall. *I won't answer*, he thought to himself. But then he did: "It's a Greek fisherman's cap. Lots of guys wear them."

"Looks like something Russian."

Nick sighed loud enough to be heard. "Well, it's not."

Jacob came on into the room and studied the cap more closely. Then his eye fell on the sign-in sheet with *Life Trust Company* at the top. Nick felt his chest tighten.

"Where did you get this?"

"There was a genetics exhibit in the lobby of the Life Trust Building, Dad. Our biology teacher wanted us to go see it and write a report. So Danny and I went down there with some girls."

"And this?" Jacob pointed again to the paper.

"We forgot to bring any paper, and the guard let us have a sheet."

"Who's your biology teacher?"

The questions were coming faster now, like gunshots.

"Cranston, Dad!"

"Cranston, huh? What did the guard say?"

Nick exploded. "Jeez, Dad, what the hell does it matter?" He was shouting. "The guard didn't say anything. Lois asked for some paper and he tore off a time sheet and gave it to us. You satisfied?"

Mother paused outside the door, then went on to the living room.

The wary smile played around Jacob's lips again, the smile that bothered Nick far more than his father's anger.

"Time is running out for me, that's what the guard was telling you."

"Oh, for cripes sake!" Nick sat down on his bed, scooted back against the wall, and placed his pillow over his stomach as though it were a shield. He wanted to stay calm, wanted to try reasoning this out, wanted to see if he couldn't reach his father through logic.

"Okay, Dad, let's play it your way. The Life Trust Company is a Commie racket and they want you out of the way because you know too much. They won't just come right out and kill you, they have to torture you first. Somehow they're sending you subtle messages. Right?"

Jacob smiled again, a cautious smile, but didn't answer.

"It was Lois who asked for the paper, not me. Somehow the guard knew who I was? Knew that Lois was with me? Knew that she was going to ask for paper, and when she did, he was supposed to hand her some time sheets? Knew that when I got mine home, you'd find it and know exactly what message they were sending this time?"

"They have our telephone bugged."

"Dad, we never discussed this over the telephone! We didn't even decide to go down to the Life Trust Building till we got to Diversey Harbor."

"They've got spies all around, Nick. The exhibit was part of their plan."

Nick felt his patience running out. It was like arguing with a small child, the kind of reasoning one got from a kindergarten pupil.

"Dad," he said at last, "do you have any idea what it would cost to arrange an exhibit in the lobby of the Life Trust Building, bug our telephone, put microphones in our medicine cabinet, have spies following us around, just to get me to go down there so the guard could give me a time sheet so I could bring it home for you to find so that you would know that time was running out?" He gave a short laugh. "Dad, why don't they just send you a postcard saying 'time is running out?'"

But Jacob wasn't laughing. "The Communists have lots of money. They'll stop at nothing." He spoke mechanically, without emotion.

"I can't believe this!" Nick said incredulously. "I can't believe that *you* believe it."

Jacob merely shrugged. His eyebrows knotted once more into a frown, as though he were intent on a conversation inside himself. Nick pressed on:

"Why would they go to all this work? I could see them doing something like this maybe to assassinate the President, but why are you so important to them?"

"I know too much."

"What do you know that the FBI doesn't?"

"I know how they operate."

Nick felt as though he were on a merry-go-round

that was going faster and faster, and he couldn't get off. He closed his eyes momentarily, trying to keep his balance, trying to think of some other way to reach this stranger who was facing him now across the room.

"Dad," he said at last, "while we were there in the lobby looking at the exhibit, I saw Mr. Connelly get off the elevator. I knew it was Connelly because I heard the guard tell him he had called a cab." His father was staring at him intently. Nick pushed on. "I've been worried about you, and I thought maybe Mr. Connelly could help. I went over to him while he was waiting and told him who I was."

The smile on Jacob's lips began again and then, just as abruptly, stopped.

"I asked him what had happened at work that made you leave."

The smile again. "And what did he tell you?"

"He said if I hadn't asked him the question, he would have asked me, because he didn't know himself."

"That's all?"

"No." Nick hesitated. He was on shaky ground, he knew. Maybe he shouldn't be talking about this. But he had begun, and he wanted his father to trust him. He wanted everything out in the open. "He said that sometime last fall you seemed upset about something and started keeping to yourself." Again

Nick paused. He could not bring himself to mention the promotion that Dad didn't get. ". . . and then, one day, you just walked out and didn't come back." He noticed that Mother had come to the door of the bedroom again. "The cab came then, and Connelly said something else. He said he felt that you needed expert help, and he wanted you to know that he wished you the very best."

Jacob's eyes narrowed. "*Expert* help!" he said, spitting out the words. "He wishes me the very best, all right."

"Nick," said his mother, "you shouldn't have said anything to Mr. Connelly."

"Then what are we going to do, Mom?" Nick said, his voice rising. "Go on living like this for the rest of our lives? Can't even make a phone call or go out the door without Dad suspecting something?"

Even as he spoke, however, Nick saw the agitation on his father's face. Jacob was pacing again, back and forth in front of Nick's window.

"*Expert* help!" he said again. "Time is running out for Jacob Karpinski."

Nick felt himself losing ground. "Dad, you've got to do what Connelly says and see a doctor. Your medical insurance will cover it."

"I don't have any medical insurance," Jacob said, as though to the window frame. "I don't work at the post office anymore. I'm not going back."

Out in the hallway, Wanda Karpinski seemed to reel. "Jacob. . . !" she said. "You told me you wanted to work for the government!"

"Not even the government can help me now," Jacob said, each word precise. "The only way I'll get out of Chicago is in a box."

"Jacob, you're sick, you're sick, you're sick!" Nick's mother put her hands on either side of her face and began to weep, stored-up gasps that couldn't seem to find their way out. Jacob turned toward her and there was a look of anguish on his own face. Wanda Karpinski noticed and flung herself through the doorway toward him. For a moment they stood there embracing in Nick's bedroom, Jacob running one hand tenderly across her back.

"I'll ask Papa for help," Mother sobbed. "I'll go to him—tell him everything. We'll get the best doctor we can find. We'll use our savings—"

Jacob straightened, and just as suddenly as he had embraced his wife, he pushed her away.

"You can't tell anyone! *Anyone!*" he scolded. "You go around talking, it'll cost me my life."

"But Jacob, that's part of the illness, can't you see? There *is* no one after you! It's all a part of the sickness."

The smile again, the smile that Nick had come to hate: "They've brainwashed you too," he said to Nick's mother, and stalked out of the room.

Mother prepared dinner that evening but Jacob pushed it aside. All evening he continued his restless pacing, his murmured mutterings, and when he tried to sit down, he could not decide which chair. He stood looking from the green to the brown, going over the choices again and again: "Green is for grass that covers the grave," he would say; "brown is the earth six feet under. . . ." And the pacing went on.

Nick turned his stereo up loud, trying to escape into his music, wanting to be carried away with the sound. Someone upstairs banged on the floor around midnight, and Nick turned the stereo off, but it was after three when he fell asleep.

He had only been asleep a few hours when he sensed the presence of someone there in his room, someone kneeling beside his bed. He struggled to open his eyes. In the half light of early dawn, he was startled to see his father's face within inches of his own. Nick bolted up on one elbow.

His father continued to crouch there by the bed. There were tears in Jacob's eyes:

"I'm sorry, Nick," he murmured. "I'm sorry that you're involved in all this. I'm so sorry. . . ."

Nick tried to make out the clock there on his desk, tried to think of an appropriate reply. But before he could collect his thoughts, Jacob went out again.

It wasn't until seven, when Nick finally got up himself, that he found the film from his camera unrolled there in the bathtub, submerged under three inches of water.

Seven

THAT HIS FATHER could be that sick, that frightened, that suspicious. . . ! Anger overwhelmed him, and Nick stumbled from the bathroom, bellowing.

"Nick. . . ?" Wanda Karpinski turned around from the stove.

"My film!" Nick stood helplessly in the hallway, staring at his father. Jacob studied him without expression from his position at the living room window.

Flinging himself toward his dad, Nick stood only inches away, fists doubled. "You ruined my film!"

"Nick! It's seven in the morning!" his mother scolded.

"My film!" Nick roared.

"I had to do it," said his father.

"*Why*?"

"There were pictures."

Nick's shoulders ached with tension: "There were pictures on there for the *yearbook*!"

"Nick, please!" said his mother.

Nick whirled about. "Don't you *care*, Mom? We spent yesterday afternoon taking pictures!" He looked about him incredulously. "This is like living in the loony bin."

A smile played on his father's face, and he sat stiffly down in the brown chair, then got up and switched to the couch.

Mrs. Karpinski came into the living room. "What did you do with his film, Jacob?"

"It's in the bathtub, Mom, under water," Nick told her, spitting out the words.

"Under *water*?"

"Of course! Makes as much sense as everything else that's happening around here!"

"Nick, stop shouting."

"What am I supposed to tell my friends? Answer that!"

"Jacob. . . ." Mrs. Karpinski faced her husband, then gave up and turned wearily toward Nick again. "I'm sorry," she said, "but right now your film is the least of my worries." And she walked on past him to the bedroom at the end of the hall.

It was like being in a play, Nick thought, where

the same scene was rehearsed again and again. *Exit Mother, stage left.*

He sat down in the chair directly across from Jacob: "Tell me straight out—what did you think was on that film?"

"*You* know," said his father.

Nick longed to leap across the room and pummel his dad with his fists. The anger almost choked him, and yet, when his father stopped smiling and his eyes took on that fearful look, Nick felt his throat constricting with sadness.

"You're sick, Dad." He couldn't deal with that now. Couldn't handle more than one emotion at a time. He went back to his own room and lay for a long time with one arm over his face. It wasn't enough to keep the secret locked up in the apartment; now he had to second-guess his father, figure out what he might do next, even up here. What would he tell Lois?

He thought of every possible explanation: *his father, not knowing the camera was loaded, exposed the film.* No way. *The camera was stolen.* No chance. *The film was ruined.* How? *The film was lost.* . . .

Nick lowered his arm and studied a crack on the ceiling. It happened all the time, didn't it? Film got sent to the wrong store . . . was misplaced in the lab . . . put in the wrong envelope . . . picked up by the wrong customer and never returned. . . . He'd buy a new roll of film and say that the lab lost the first one.

The bedroom door opened and Mother came in, closing it after her. She leaned against the wall:

"I just wanted you to know that I'm going to talk with Father Thomas about using St. John's for my piano lessons. There's a fairly good piano in the side chapel. I tried it. I'm going to see if he'll let me rent the chapel after school and on Saturday mornings."

"You going to tell him about Dad?"

She sighed. "Sometime, maybe—when Jacob's ready."

"How ready do you want him, Mom? You waiting for him to do something *really* weird?"

"I want him to *know* he's sick."

Nick sat up and swung his legs over the side of the bed. "He *can't*, Mom! That's part of the sickness. It's everybody else, not him."

"Give me time, Nick. The first thing is to find another place to teach. We've got to have money; our savings won't last forever, but I simply can't go on giving lessons here. The students are beginning to notice. Once I've worked that out, then we'll see what's next."

Nick could understand that, all right. Each day he mentally lined up his problems to see what deserved the lion's share of worry. No contest. Dad always took first place.

Nick went to the deli around noon to pick up some lunch. Standing in front of the potato salad with his mother's list, he pointed to the antipasto, then the sausages, and Mr. Perona packaged them for him.

"Try our new dip," the man said. "Here, I'll put some on a cracker."

"What's in it?"

Perona laughed. "Three secret ingredients, and every one of 'em's garlic. You're Polish? You'll love it."

Nick grinned and took the cracker. The dip was strong and utterly delicious.

"See? What did I tell you?" Perona said.

The door opened and Karen Zimmerman came in, humming to herself in her funny little way.

Oh, Jeez! Nick thought. He swallowed and tried to wash off his teeth with his tongue.

"Hi, Nick," she said, coming over.

"Hi." Nick kept one hand next to his mouth. Even the fingers that had held the cracker reeked of garlic.

"It's so nice outside!" she said. "This has been the most beautiful weekend!"

"Sure has," said Nick, facing the other way. He could tell, however, that Karen was looking at him strangely.

"Nick?" she said, coming closer. "You mad at me or something?"

"Mad? Me?" The color rose to Nick's face. He

turned, backing up to keep his distance, and half-stumbled over a bag of hazelnuts there on the floor. "Why should I be mad?"

Karen stopped in her tracks. She looked from him to Mr. Perona, and suddenly Perona burst out laughing.

"Here," he said, handing Karen a cracker with the garlic dip. "What Nick's got, it's catching."

"Oh, wow!" Karen said as she bit into it. Then she laughed too.

Nick came over then. "Didn't want to blow you away."

"No chance."

"You here for lunch?"

"Breakfast. The Zimmermans sleep late on Sundays."

"Yeah," Nick smiled. "We do, too."

The smile lasted until he got back home. The air *was* balmy, like Karen said. Halfway up the stairs, however, Nick stopped suddenly and sat down. A heavy kind of sadness came over him.

He didn't know what had set him off this time—the pretense, perhaps, that his family was just like Karen's—normal, happy people who slept late on Sunday and picked up something from the deli. "The Zimmermans," Karen had said, like she was proud of them, glad to be included.

It was the good times he'd had with his father that haunted Nick now, more intense in the remembering, perhaps, than they had actually been—the birthdays, the traditional hike after Thanksgiving dinner, the season tickets to the White Sox games, camping. . . . But these were mostly scheduled activities—projects that had to be planned. Jacob Karpinski did not take to things spontaneously.

Your father has never been easy to get close to. Mr. Connelly's words came back to Nick now.

He leads his life, I lead mine. Uncle Thad.

Maybe no one could get close to Jacob, not really. And the thought that perhaps the good times, what there had been of them, were over, that there was nothing better down the road, upset Nick more than he had counted on. Sadness, regret—love, even— were far more unwieldy feelings than anger.

"I don't know what's keeping him. . . ." Nick heard his mother's voice from the top of the stairs as she came out into the hall. He grabbed the sack there by his feet and went on up to the apartment.

That night, behind his closed door, Nick carefully built a scaffolding out of books. On the very top he placed his pencil box and a small round tin of marbles. If anyone opened his door in the middle of the night, Nick wanted to know.

DANNY BECK had a favor to ask. He cornered Nick in the locker room Monday after gym.

"Listen," he said earnestly, giving his curly hair the once-over with the towel. "I got a problem. Karen wants us all to come over to her apartment a week from Saturday. But I've got a date with a girl in my church."

"So?" Nick buckled his belt. "Just tell Karen you've got other plans. You're not engaged or anything."

"Are you crazy?" Danny said. "She might not go to the spring semi-formal with me if she finds out."

"Well, if you're so worried about Karen, how come you're dating another girl?"

"Just want to have a back-up in case anything happens between Karen and me."

Nick stared at him in amazement. "You are one weird fella, you know it?"

"Look, Nick. Tickets to the dance are ten bucks, and you have to buy them two weeks in advance. Anything could happen between Karen and me in two weeks."

"When's the dance?"

"May second."

"Ye gods, Danny! This is only March!"

"I like to be prepared."

Nick sat down and thrust one foot in his sneaker. "I don't believe this. I stick around you long enough, Danny, we'll both be nuts." He laughed.

"Listen. All I want is for you and Lois to go over to Karen's a week from Saturday and make some excuse for me."

"No way. I'll go to Karen's, but you've got to make your own excuses," Nick told him.

"Okay, okay. So I'm cautious! So I'm a nerd! Ten bucks is a lot of money."

Nick smiled and shook his head. "You're a real case, buddy."

He had a test to make up over the lunch hour, so he did not see his friends in the cafeteria. In biology, Lois called across the room: "Nick, when will we see the pictures?"

"Probably tomorrow," he told her.

His mind wandered in and out of Cranston's lecture. If he picked up a roll of film on the way home, he could take his camera to school the next day, tell them that Walgreens couldn't find the pictures, that they'd better take some more, just in case.

When school let out, he swiftly got his jacket from his locker and started off ahead of the crowd. When he got to the corner, however, he heard Karen calling. He stopped and waited.

"I've been trying to catch up for a whole block," she said breathlessly, one hand over her heart. "You in training or something?"

He smiled. "You should have yelled."

They waited for the light, then crossed.

"How about coming over a week from Saturday?" she said, as he knew she would. "I've already asked

Danny and Lois. We can rent a movie for the VCR, and Mom's going to make chocolate fondue. Seven-thirty okay?"

"Sure."

"Good. Mom's been after me to invite you all over. She says I'm too much of a loner."

"You? A loner?"

Karen laughed. "Mother thinks so. She says I don't go out of my way to make friends the way my sisters did."

Nick smiled at her. "Seems to me you can attract enough friends without going out of your way at all."

"That was the perfect answer, Nick Karpinski! I'll tell Mom you said that." Karen pulled off her knit cap and let her long hair slide down her neck to her shoulders. "Spring!" she said, tilting her face up toward the sun. "The only thing I hate about Chicago is the winter. How about you?"

"Oh, Chicago's okay," Nick told her. "I've only been here a couple years."

"That's what I thought. But Lois said she couldn't remember you at all last year." Karen stopped suddenly and slapped one hand over her mouth. "Oh, my gosh, that sounded awful."

Nick laughed out loud. "It's okay. Before this year I was sort of out to lunch."

This time she laughed. "What's that supposed to mean?"

"Oh, I just felt out of things, I guess. Didn't know anybody. It takes a while."

Karen nodded. "Mother's always pushing me to go out and *meet* people. She thinks you can just pick friends up off the street like gum wrappers or something. Anyway, I can remember the day you moved in."

"You can?" Nick glanced over at her.

"It was a freezing Saturday in January, and when Mother saw you—I think you were carrying a gerbil cage or something— she said, 'Now *there's* a friend for you, Karen.' That's why I've been avoiding you for a whole year."

Nick grinned.

When he got up to the apartment, it was strangely quiet, and he remembered that his mother was giving lessons now over at St. John's. He felt uneasy coming home alone to his father, not sure of what he would find. What he found was Jacob waiting for him at the top of the stairs.

"Who were you talking to?" Jacob demanded, following him inside. "I could hear you down in the lobby."

A secret agent, Nick wanted to say, but played it straight: "A girl who lives on the other side of the building." He hung up his jacket.

"What's her name?"

"What difference does it make, Dad?"

"What's her *name*?" Jacob insisted.

"Karen Zimmerman." Nick started back to his room, but something about his father's face stopped him. Jacob's skin looked pale. There were rings about his eyes from lack of sleep, and when he talked, his lips stuck to dry teeth.

"Nick, they've got a contract out on me. I need protection."

How should he answer? Play the game? Show him how ridiculous it sounded?

"I don't know what to say to you, Dad," Nick ventured at last. "No one's after you, but you can't seem to believe that."

Perspiration stood out on Jacob's forehead, and it seemed to Nick as though, in spite of the wrinkles, his father had grown suddenly very young—a small, terrified child imprisoned in a man's body. Nick himself felt like this child's keeper. He had to take care of his dad, keep the fear contained, his father in the house, and the secret of Dad's illness safely under lock and key. Keep it from his friends, anyway.

"Dad, I want to help, if you'd just let me!"

"I believe you, Nick. I know you would. They just won't allow it, that's all."

"I want you to go see a doctor. Any doctor you like."

"No! A doctor won't help. They'd pump me full of drugs—get me addicted, turn me into a zombie. They've bribed the doctors, Nick."

Nick drew in his breath, held it, then let it out again. "Scratch the doctors," he murmured, and went on back to his room. There was an ache inside him that he couldn't handle, and he pressed his palms against his ears to block out his father's footsteps, pacing the hall. Whatever it was that Jacob feared, the fear itself was real—as excruciating a pain, Nick knew, as he could imagine. How must it feel not to be believed by your own family? To feel that you were about to die, yet the others were going on about their business? No matter how desperately Nick wanted to help, there was a wall between him and his father that he couldn't get around or through or over.

WHEN MOTHER came home about six, Nick had put in the meat loaf she'd left for supper along with three potatoes to bake. Jacob, however, would not even sit down.

Halfway through dinner, he came to the kitchen doorway and announced, "I need the help of the Catholic Church."

Nick and his mother looked at each other. Mrs. Karpinski put down her fork. "What, Jacob?"

Jacob leaned over the table, whispering across the salad. "They're the only ones who can help me now. When you go to a church and ask for refuge, they have to take you in."

Nick stopped eating. His mother skidded back in her chair.

"Jacob," she said, "will you go talk with Father Thomas?"

Nick wished she had not put it in the form of a question. He got up from the table, leaving his own dinner half-eaten.

"Let's go, Dad. Let's go see the priest and tell him everything. Okay? You said you needed protection. Let's go."

Jacob was breathing jerkily, his face looked even paler than before. He looked from one to the other uncertainly.

"I'll get my purse," Mother said, hurrying.

Guiding his father toward the door, Nick got Jacob's jacket from the hall closet. Jacob plunged one hand again and again toward the armhole before he got it in.

Halfway down the stairs, Nick's father pulled out his car keys.

"You don't need those, Jacob," Mrs. Karpinski said. "St. John's is just down the block."

"I'll drive," Jacob said, and his voice had turned sullen. Nick felt his stomach flip-flop.

"Well, all right then, we'll go in style!" Mother said with forced gaiety, and they all went around to the park in back and got in the front seat of the Pontiac, Mother in the middle.

Always before, Nick had felt safe in the car, protected by his father's expert driving. Now, for the first time, he was uneasy.

At the corner, Jacob turned right instead of left.

"The church is *that* way, Jacob!" Mother said.

But the car kept going. Nick sat motionless while the wipers swept rhythmically at a light drizzle.

They drove around for a half hour. At every corner there was a new decision to be made, Nick knew, and he could almost hear his father's thoughts: Should he turn left or right? Go forward or back? Even the street names had probably taken on political significance: Montrose, Addison, Western, Sunset Ridge . . . all had meanings that had to be deciphered, and sometimes the Pontiac would start to turn left, then veer sharply to the right; other times they would sit so long at a stop sign that cars behind would begin honking. Sweat broke out again on Jacob's forehead.

"Dad, I've got homework to do," Nick said at last, when a clock at a service station read seven forty-five.

But his father did not answer, and the Pontiac rolled on.

"Jacob, where are we going?" Mother said wearily, too exhausted now to argue. "You said you wanted to talk with Father Thomas."

"*You* said that," Jacob told her. "That's the whole idea, isn't it? To get me out of the apartment? They know I'm coming."

Mother covered her face with her hands and

began to cry. "I can't take anymore, Jacob. I just c . . . can't. Please drive us home."

But if Nick's father heard, he gave no answer. Then, finally, "I want to become a priest."

Nick heard words but didn't react to them any longer. Comments went from paranoid to ludicrous. He was becoming so used to hearing the bizarre that the sentences rolled off him now as though he were shock-repellent.

"There's a rectory somewhere north of here, I've seen it," Jacob said. "If they'll take me in, I'm staying."

Wanda Karpinski turned and stared at him. "What about us?"

"*You'll* be okay. *They'll* see to that."

"My god!" Mother whispered. Nick felt like a mechanical man, wound up so tight that the spring was broken. He couldn't even move. Could not even feel his chest give when he breathed.

They passed a bank and Nick was surprised to see that it was after nine. He seemed to have lost all track of time. Then they passed a Walgreens and he remembered the film he had forgotten to buy. He stared dully through the glass, experimenting with closing his eyelids halfway, forcing long yellow streaks to radiate out from the headlights of oncoming cars. When he stopped squinting, the streaks disappeared.

They were arguing now, his parents. Wanda was

indignant. "You have a wife and son to think about, Jacob! You haven't worked for weeks! There are bills to pay! Who's going to make you a priest?"

"I need protection," Jacob said. The merry-go-round was going faster, spinning out of control.

"Well, so do we!" Mother was screaming. Screaming and sobbing at the same time. "Protection from you, Jacob!" And then her voice softened and she leaned her head against him. "Oh, Jacob, we need help!"

And Jacob, in turn, was sympathetic. "I know, Wanda. I've been trying to tell you. Don't worry. I'll soon be out of the house, and you won't be in danger anymore. I'm sorry. I'm so sorry."

Mother had fallen into the trap. Nick could see how easy it was to do that, to let Dad twist your meaning until you found yourself talking his language. One word, and your feet slid out from under you. Two words, and you felt yourself falling. And then you were down in the pit wondering how you got there. It didn't help to remain neutral, either, or even to keep quiet. These only seemed to upset Jacob further.

The same buildings began to appear for a second and third time outside the window. Nick looked down at his watch in the darkness. The numbers read nine thirty-two. His legs began to cramp.

"Jacob," Mother said, "dinner is still sitting out on the table at home. Let's go back."

No answer. The Great Stone Face behind the wheel gave no response.

Nick wondered if maybe, when they reached the next stop sign, he should just open the door and get out. Go call Uncle Thad. Then he wondered if he should leave Mother alone in the car with Dad. He thought not.

He leaned back against the seat and closed his eyes, thinking about the assignments he hadn't even started, the English theme he was supposed to write.

Okay, Nick, what's your excuse this time?

Just out looking for a rectory, Mrs. Saunders; my Dad wants to be a priest.

He must have dozed off, because when the Pontiac stopped at last, it took Nick a moment or two to figure out where he was. He leaned forward and squinted out the window.

They had found the rectory. The Pontaic was parked in the circular drive of a large house with a stone cross above the entrance. Except for a lamp burning just inside the glass doors, the windows of the house were dark.

His father got out and took the keys, and when the door slammed behind him, Nick heard his mother weeping softly. He didn't know how to comfort her; he couldn't even comfort himself. He raised one arm and put it around her shoulder.

On the steps, Jacob was ringing the doorbell. His hair looked disheveled. Scarcely had he dropped his hand from the bell than he raised it again and rang a second time. Then, without waiting, he began to bang on the door, looking around anxiously as though any minute Russian soldiers might spring up out of the bushes.

A second light came on inside as the figure of a man moved slowly down the hallway toward the door. At the window, the priest stopped and peered out. At first Nick thought he might not let Jacob in, but then the door opened.

Wanda Karpinski sat up and watched. Jacob was saying something. The priest said something. Then Jacob was talking again. The priest stepped out on the porch and looked intently at the Pontiac there in the drive. Finally, holding the door open, he ushered Nick's father inside.

Eight

WHEN THE RECTORY DOOR closed behind Jacob, Mother's sobs erupted full force, as though all the tears she'd been holding back were making their escape. Nick sat miserably on the seat beside her.

"Well, Mom, at least he's talking to somebody," he ventured at last.

Her shoulders continued to shake. "I'm so humiliated."

"Why?"

"He's a *husband*, Nick. A *father*! That he should want to leave us and become a priest!"

"But Mom, he's sick! You know that!"

"That he should tell them, though." The weeping went on.

Nick waited while she cried herself out. Finally,

when the tears had stopped, she fumbled about in her purse for a tissue and said, "It's time. We've got to get him into a hospital. We can't go on like this—I see that now."

At last. Nick felt as though a valve had been opened in his head, and all the steam and impatience and anger had dissipated. They were still a team—he and Mom, at least; together they'd do what needed to be done.

"We'll get along somehow, Mom," he said encouragingly. His thoughts tumbled on ahead of him, making plans. "Maybe you could take driving lessons. It'll be three years yet before I get my license. We may need the car. . . ."

The thought perturbed her, however; he could tell.

"I've got enough things to worry about without that," she said. "I had to do the income tax myself last week. I can't take on the driving too." She was weeping again. "It's hard, when I've depended so on Jacob."

"Well, he's come this far," Nick answered. "Maybe the priests can help."

Mother dabbed at her eyes. "At least they'll know what to do, won't they, Nick? They have contacts. They know the best doctors."

"Can we afford the best doctors, Mom?"

"We still have some bonds. Jacob was always very

good at investing. But if I have to, I'll ask Papa for money."

"I could get a part-time job," Nick offered.

"That might help," Mother said. "This has been hard on you too, though."

The time dragged on—thirty minutes, forty. The car grew colder.

"Perhaps they didn't realize we were out here," Mother said finally. "What if they put him to bed and are planning to talk with him again in the morning?"

Nick peered through the darkness. "Maybe I should go check."

They debated some more, waited some more, then saw the silhouette of the priest coming through the hallway once again. He came outside and walked down the steps toward the car. Mother rolled down the window.

"Mrs. Karpinski?" The priest bent down, his eyes scanning the front seat, settling first on her, then on Nick, then back to Mother again.

"Yes?" Mother said.

"I've been talking to your husband. . . ." The priest hesitated. "I'm sure you realize that Jacob is a very sick man."

"Yes, Father, I know."

"How long has he been this way?"

"Over three months now."

120

"He needs far more help than we can give him. He is very anxious, very distraught, and right now I think he needs protection from his own fears. You should think about getting him into a hospital."

Do something, the priest seemed to be saying.

"Have you any suggestions?" Mrs. Karpinski asked.

Someone else was coming out the door now, a second priest, one arm about Jacob.

The man at the window lowered his voice a little. "Is he a veteran?"

"Yes."

"Maybe the VA would admit him. It's worth a try." The priest straightened up and opened the car door for Jacob. He reached out and shook his hand. Stiffly, without a word, Nick's father slid onto the seat beside Mother and the door closed after him.

"Good luck, Jacob. Let us know how things come out," the second priest said from the steps.

Still there was no answer. Jacob turned the key in the ignition, the motor started up, and then the Pontiac moved forward again, rolling off into nowhere, without plans or destination.

The air was heavy with disappointment.

"What did they say, Jacob?" Mrs. Karpinski asked.

"They won't take me. They don't want to get involved."

Nick closed his eyes, feeling dull, lifeless.

"Jacob, did they talk to you about entering a hospital?" Mother asked.

Nick's father gave a low laugh. "A *hospital*!" The words came out in a snarl. "That's right where the Commies want me. They want to fill me full of drugs. They put me in a hospital, Wanda, I'll never get out."

"Jacob, that's not true!"

But the Pontiac headed home.

"I'm tired," said Jacob. Wordlessly they parked, wordlessly they each got out and made the silent trek upstairs to the apartment. Nothing had changed, nothing at all.

NICK SAT in a chair just inside Miss Etting's office and waited until she had examined a girl behind the screen.

"Just a sprain, I think," the nurse said, as they came back around, the girl leaning on her, "but I think you should have it X-rayed. Use the phone here to call your mother. Tell her you'll need help getting out to the car." She glanced over at Nick. "Be with you in a minute."

The girl hobbled over to the desk and made the call while Miss Etting signed a readmission slip for a boy waiting by the door.

"Grand Central, this morning," the nurse said and then, to Nick, "Let's go to my inner sanctum."

They went inside the adjoining room and Miss Etting closed the door after them.

It was a small room, snug, without windows. Baskets of plants hung from the ceiling at one end, beneath a special light, and beneath the plants, two comfortable chairs, facing each other. At the other end of the room was a cot with a blanket folded neatly at the bottom.

Nick sat down and Miss Etting faced him. This time she said nothing at all, just waited for Nick to begin, never taking her eyes off him.

"It's about this friend, again," Nick said, and she nodded. "He called last night. His father isn't getting any better, and yesterday he did something really strange. He drove his wife and son around Chicago for a couple hours and then tried to become a priest."

Miss Etting's brows knit ever so slightly on her forehead. "How?" she asked.

"He drove to a rectory and asked the Fathers to take him in. A priest came out to the car later and told his wife that the man should be hospitalized, but they didn't say how to get him there. They said try the veterans' hospital."

"He's a veteran, this man?"

"Yeah, I guess so." Nick wondered for a moment if he was telling too much. "My friend was wondering how you get someone into the hospital when he doesn't want to go?"

"The sixty-four thousand dollar question," Miss

Etting said, and stared thoughtfully at the opposite wall.

"My friend thought the priests would do something. That they'd help get his father hospitalized. They didn't."

"They couldn't," said Miss Etting. "Not unless the man was clearly a danger to himself or to someone else."

Nick felt a trace of anger. The last time he had talked to the nurse, she had stressed the importance of getting the mother to realize that her husband was ill, of *doing* something. Now she seemed to be saying that nothing could be done.

"So how *do* you get someone in the hospital?"

"I wish I had an easy answer," Miss Etting said. "As far as I know, if a person won't admit himself voluntarily, then he has to be committed. I think that two psychiatrists have to examine him and declare him mentally ill."

"How do you get him to the psychiatrists?" Nick sensed the impatience in his own voice.

Miss Etting dropped her hands helplessly in her lap. "I don't know. Is there a family doctor who could help? Maybe the mother could get her husband to him, and then he could call in two psychiatrists. It would be terribly upsetting, I know. . . ."

"And . . . if he hasn't done anything dangerous enough yet to be committed, then they just have to wait until he *does*?"

"I think that's the way it is, Nick. It's not fair, I know, but if you were able to commit people just because a relative *said* he might do something, think of the trouble that might cause. All I can really suggest is to start with the family doctor. . . ."

The hanging plants seemed to become a jungle in front of Nick's eyes, the leaves twisting and turning and shutting out the light. Nick felt he had lost his way and saw no path out of the maze.

"Bad news. Walgreens lost my film."

Nick flung the words out over the table in the cafeteria like cards, wanting to be done with them.

The others paused, sandwiches held halfway to their mouths.

"Oh, Nick!" Lois cried in disappointment.

Nick fumbled with his milk carton, splashing drops as he worked it open and thrust his straw inside. "Wouldn't you know? They've put a tracer on it and said to call back tomorrow. But I'll pick up another roll of film after school, and we could take some more pictures then."

"It wouldn't be the same," Lois said sulkily.

"I've got soccer practice," said Danny.

Karen didn't say anything at all.

"Then I'll bring my camera tomorrow and we can take the pictures over the lunch hour," Nick said. "I'll ask for one-day service, and we'll still make the deadline on Friday."

"It's worth a try," Karen said hopefully.

"I just *knew* this would happen!" Lois complained. "I *knew* it!" She wasn't exactly glaring at Nick, but it was the next thing to it. "We went to all that work. . . !"

"I'm sorry," Nick said.

"You should have taken them somewhere else," Lois went on. "Walgreens always louses up."

It didn't feel like April, it felt like January. Karen had orchestra rehearsal after school, so Nick didn't even have her company on the way home. Lois walked with him as far as the el, but Nick almost wished she hadn't. She was sullen and uncommunicative, and when he said, "See you tomorrow," she didn't even respond. He almost forgot to pick up the second roll of film at Walgreens, then went back for it. This time, when he got to the apartment, he hid both his camera and the film in the bottom of his school bag.

Wednesday, however, was dark. The rain began at seven that morning and came down in sheets. For a time it looked as though the sky might clear around eleven, then it darkened and by noon it was raining again.

Nick and the others had brought their funny caps for the pictures just in case, but there wasn't enough light indoors and Nick didn't have a flash. Lois walked out of the cafeteria in disgust.

Karen gave Nick a sardonic smile. "She'll get over it," she told him.

If there was one thing Nick had learned, though, it was that whenever he thought things couldn't get worse, they did. He arrived home at three to find that his father had moved the refrigerator in front of the kitchen door leading out to the fire escape.

"What's that for?" Nick asked, staring.

"Protection," his father said.

"Dad, if there's a fire, we can't get out."

"If there's a fire, we can move it, but *they* can't," Jacob replied.

His illness took an even sharper twist that evening.

"Why don't you just turn me over to them right now?"

The words came halfway through supper, between the end of the salad and the beginning of the baked fish. Nick did not think he could take it. Jacob was like a record, endlessly repeating. The same tone, the same accusations, the same look, over and over, night after night. Not only was it ridiculous, it was boring. Didn't Dad ever get tired of it, too?

The platter paused in Mother's hands. "What?"

"How much are they paying you to turn me in?" Jacob went on. "Thirty pieces of silver, huh? That's all I'm worth to you. Thirty pieces of silver?"

"Jacob, what. . . ?"

Jacob got up from the table, went to the bedroom,

and returned with a small cosmetic bag, which he slapped down onto the table. Mother blanched. A handful of crumpled five and ten dollar bills fell out, along with several silver dollars. "I found it in the closet," he said coldly, 'behind the extra pillow."

Nick shut his eyes, hands gripping the table. But it was Mother, unexpectedly, who exploded in anger.

"Yes, I hid that, Jacob! Because I'm worried! Because I want to have something put away. No telling *what* you'll do next. It's two days of teaching money, that's all it is. Look at it yourself. If the Communists are going to pay me to get rid of you, they can certainly offer more than thirty-two dollars and fifty cents."

Once more she had fallen into his trap, Nick thought. Now Mother was keeping secrets. Now Dad had her talking about the Communists as well. How easy it was to do!

"How much more?" The odd smile was twisting Jacob's lips as he hovered over her. It was the smile Nick hated more than anything else. "What did the Commies offer you? A thousand? A million?"

"Do you really think you are worth a million dollars to them, Jacob?" Mother cried, oblivious to the senselessness of the argument. "Where do you get these delusions? What could you possibly know that would make you so valuable?"

Jacob merely nodded his head and went on smiling.

"Answer me!" Wanda Karpinski suddenly lunged from her chair and grabbed hold of his shirt, angry tears flashing in her eyes, her face strangely pink. And then, when he went on smiling, she clawed at him, screaming, "*Answer* me! What makes you so damned important that they have to do this to you? *Tell* me!" Now, at last, she was crying.

Calmly, coldly, Jacob detached her fingers from his shirt, and when Mother sank back into her chair, hands over her face, Jacob turned to Nick and said quietly, "She's the sick one, Nick, not me."

Leaping up from the table, Nick raced through the living room and out the door, unable to stand it any longer. He fantasied just packing up some night, he and Mom, and moving to another apartment— even going back to South Bend. But even as he thought it, he knew he wanted to save them all, not only Mom and himself, but Jacob.

He went out to the park in back and stood shivering there on the sidewalk. He toyed with the idea of going to St. John's and bringing Father Thomas back with him—showing him what was happening there at home. But what would the priest see? A man and his wife eating supper. Would Jacob repeat his accusations in front of Father Thomas? No. He would be calm and very, very rational. Dad would tell the priest that he had walked in on a family quarrel and to please come back another time.

Thrusting his hands in his pants pockets, Nick

walked down the street toward Walgreens to get warm. As he passed the deli, however, he remembered the "Help Wanted" sign he had seen in the window the week before. He retraced his steps. The sign was gone. He went inside anyway.

"I don't know, Nick," said Mr. Perona, pushing a salami through the slicing machine. "Hired a boy last week and he didn't work out. Late the first two days and the third day he didn't show at all. I've got to have somebody reliable." He scowled at Nick over his glasses.

"I'm reliable," Nick told him. "You wouldn't have any problems with me."

Perona studied him. "This your first job?" His eyes quickly scanned Nick's bare arms.

Nick nodded. *Jeez*, he thought, he'd gone off without his jacket. Hadn't brushed his teeth, either. Combed his hair. Must look to Perona like a spur-of-the-moment decision. It was.

"Don't mind scrubbing floors, unloading trucks, washing dishes, cleaning windows. . . ?"

"I can do anything you've got," Nick said hopefully.

Perona scowled some more. "It'll be two hours after school every day plus Saturdays. That's not going to interfere with anything now, is it? Don't go quitting on me after a couple weeks."

"That would be great," Nick said. He could hardly believe it. Some things might be going wrong in his life, but not everything. He ran back home, almost forgetting what had gone on only a half hour before.

When he walked back in the apartment, the quarrel was over. Jacob was in the living room, reading the paper in the manner he'd adopted lately, a few lines at a time, then a glance around the apartment, a few lines more, another glance. Like the beacon in a lighthouse, Nick thought, always searching something out. He went on into the kitchen where Mother was putting the supper things away.

"I've got a job, Mom!"

Wanda Karpinski turned around, her eyes still red. "Nick, where on earth did you go? I didn't know if you'd finished or not."

"I got a job!" Nick repeated. "I talked to Mr. Perona at the deli. Two hours a day after school and Saturdays."

"Nick, that's wonderful!" his mother said, hesitantly. "You're sure you can handle it with all your schoolwork?"

"I can do it. Don't worry."

"It's going to help. It really will."

Nick stepped back into the living room, almost daring his father to say something. He was feeling strong, ready for a confrontation, if necessary. But Jacob avoided his eyes and sat staring down at the newspaper. He wasn't reading, Nick knew. He could tell the way the eyes did not move along the print but fixed themselves on one particular spot. The pang, again. The awful longing for a dad he could share things with. Nick went down the hall to his room and closed the door.

No, Nick reported to his friends on Thursday, the pictures were never found, but Lois seemed resigned to it and Danny had lost interest. Nick went to the deli after school, and for two hours stood at the sink in the back room scouring pans. He was unaccustomed to bending over and his back and shoulders ached, but in spite of his fatigue, Nick went home at five o'clock whistling.

When he got to the apartment, however, he found the door chained. Nick swallowed, and it felt like an ice cube going down his throat. He didn't need this —not today, not when he was already dog-tired. He was sick of being Dad's keeper.

"Dad?" He put his mouth to the opening and called again. "Dad?"

Nick could see only a little way into the apartment through the one-inch crack. He searched for some sign of his father—sprawled on the floor, perhaps. He sniffed the air for the smell of gas. Nothing.

"Dad?" he called again. "It's Nick."

No answer.

Nick sat down on the top step, just outside the door, and let out his breath, slowly. Now what? Call Mr. Schmidt? The police? Was this what he had been waiting for, the outrageous act that would convince a doctor that Jacob needed to be hospitalized? Even as he sat there thinking, another part of him wondered why he wasn't trying to get in, why he wasn't making every second count, why he wasn't going for help. . . . The everyday sounds of voices and footsteps in the lobby below seemed an eerie counterpoint to the silence inside the apartment. Nick imagined Mr. Schmidt coming upstairs and sawing through the chain; imagined the police breaking the door down, the crowd gathering in the hallway outside, his father's body. . . .

Nick leaped up suddenly, his palms wet, and tried slipping his hand through the crack to release the chain, but it wouldn't work. One of the screws on the chain plate was loose, however, and Nick found that by reaching a finger inside and rubbing along one edge of the screw, he could dislodge it. The screw fell onto the parquet floor.

Frantically, Nick pulled the door shut, then banged it open again with all his strength, pushing against the taut chain. The remaining screw began to loosen. Again and again, Nick closed the door, then thrust it open against the chain, pulling the second screw out a little way with each thrust. His heart pounded violently and his breathing came shakily. He wanted to cry but he couldn't. The door across the hallway opened just a crack, an eye peered out, then the door closed again. Nick gave one final shove to the door, and this time the screw pulled out enough that Nick could touch it with his finger, and he twisted it out as he'd done the first. The metal plate dropped off the doorframe and clanked against the door.

Inside the apartment, he looked quickly around for his father.

"Dad . . ." he called again, but there was scarcely any volume to his voice. His lips were dry.

The living room was empty. He checked the study. Empty. As Nick started down the hall, Jacob appeared in the doorway at the end.

Nick leaned heavily against the wall, trying to get his breath. "Why didn't you answer the door?" he asked finally, relief and resentment flowing through his veins.

Jacob started toward him but didn't answer, and Nick grabbed his sleeve as his father passed.

"Why did you chain the door? I was about to go get Mr. Schmidt or something."

"You got in," was all Jacob said.

"I had to pull the chain off," Nick yelled. "Didn't you hear me? What were you doing, anyway?"

Jacob walked over to the door and peered down at the dangling chain, then went furtively over to the windows and examined the locks.

Not trusting himself to say more, Nick hung up his jacket and took his books into his room. A few minutes later, however, when his father went into the bathroom, Nick slipped down the hall to his parents' bedroom and looked around.

The light was still on by the desk and some papers protruded from a drawer. Nick walked over and pulled them out.

On the first paper was a meticulously drawn map of the neighborhood with X's on certain locations— Schmidt's apartment, the Zimmerman's apartment, Walgreen's, St. John's, the Becks'. . . . Anyone they knew by name was located on the map. By the X over the deli, Jacob had written, *Perona.*

Nick quickly scanned the second sheet. It was a drawing of the Karpinski apartment, with every door and window marked, and what appeared to be distances between doors and windows, carefully measured, as well as the approximate distance from windows to the ground below.

Down the hall, the toilet flushed, and Nick stuffed the papers back in the drawer the way he had found them and went out to the kitchen.

Mechanically he went through the ritual of setting the table for dinner. They were all there on the map —his friends, his employer, his school, a few of Mother's friends. . . . Nick knew without asking; that was the enemies list, and the second map was Jacob's own escape plan. Who knew what he might do next? There were a hundred possibilities, each worse than the one before, yet nothing Jacob had done so far was enough to get him hospitalized. So he had chained the door. So he had drawn a map of the neighborhood. You couldn't commit a man for that.

In a sudden frenzy, Nick went back to the living room and attacked the second chain plate on the back of the door with a screwdriver. When the whole apparatus fell off in his hand, he took the door chain out into the hall and dropped it down the incinerator.

Even as he did so Nick wondered if, secretly, almost unconsciously, he wished that he had found his father dead in the back bedroom, and that the nightmare at last were over.

Nine

WHEN NICK WOKE the next morning, he fought it, and tried to slip back into his cocoon of sleep—tried to submerge himself once more into some wisp of a dream and delay, for a few minutes, even, the dull chronic dread that greeted him now when he opened his eyes.

Spring had settled down on Chicago seemingly overnight, however, and buds had grown fat on the branches. The first green curls of new leaves gave the pear tree in the courtyard a feathery look. Always before, Nick had felt exhilarated by spring —the prelude to summer, which he loved. In the last few months, however, he had got over looking forward to anything. And on this day, when Nick went off to school and then to his job at the deli, he braced himself once again for what he might find at home afterwards.

What he found was Jacob sitting motionless in the living room listening to music. It was the same recording, over and over again, that he had been playing on and off all week, Mozart's Requiem—somber, mournful music that gave the apartment the feel of a funeral parlor. There were tears in Jacob's eyes as he listened, but when Nick spoke to him, he turned away. Nick went on back to his room.

"What's with the music?" Nick asked his mother that evening when the record stopped and Jacob started it playing all over again.

Mother kept her back to him this time as she answered, and her voice sounded thick: "You know what a requiem is, Nick."

"A mass for the dead, right?"

"He feels it's prophetic, somehow."

Nick didn't want to hear anymore about his father's prophecies. Jacob always started at the wrong end of worry. He began first with the outcome and then made up the warnings to fit it. But Mother went on:

"There's a story about Mozart," she said as she rinsed the plates for the dishwater. "When he was still a young man, he became obsessed with death, the way Jacob is. One day a stranger commissioned him to write a mass, and Mozart was sure that this was a message warning him of his own death. And he died before the mass was finished."

138

The words slipped from Nick's mouth before he could stop them: "So he's Mozart now, huh? First he's so important that the Communists would pay a million dollars to get rid of him, then he accuses you of turning him in for thirty pieces of silver, like Judas and Jesus Christ, and now he's Mozart." He had thought he was merely making an observation, but Mother turned on him.

"Isn't there any compassion in you at all?"

Her words stung. It seemed strange she should even ask—that she couldn't tell just by looking. His whole body, he felt sometimes, was one big lump of sadness, as though he were always holding back tears.

"Mom, of course! But if we're so compassionate, why aren't we *doing* something? How long do you think I can go on hiding him like this—not telling my friends, not telling the neighbors, making excuses. . . ."

The music in the next room stopped abruptly. Jacob glared at them as he passed the kitchen and went into the bathroom, slamming the door behind him.

"Listen, Nick." Mrs. Karpinski sat down at the table across from him. "I've spent every morning this week down at the drugstore making phone calls."

"I'm sorry. . . ." He was. He and Mom lashed out

at each other sometimes when it was Jacob they were angry with. "It just seems as though *some-one—*"

"Someone can wave a magic wand and get him into a hospital?" Mother gave a bitter laugh. "That's what the woman at the Family Service Agency said when I called her. 'Do you really think,' she asked, 'that we can *force* your husband to admit himself?' "

Nick remembered Miss Etting's advice about the family doctor. "What about Dr. Loring? Maybe he could help."

"He hardly knows us, Nick. I couldn't get Jacob in there, and even if I could, do you think he would really tell the doctor what he's worried about?"

"*You* could go talk to him, Mom. Ask him to make a house call."

"Nick, I've only seen the man a few times myself. He doesn't know a thing about us, really. What if he *did* come here? What would he see? You think he's going to put Jacob in the hospital just because he's out of work and looking worried? Jacob wouldn't go! How would he get him there?"

"Mom, people are placed on mental wards every day; you can't tell me they all admitted themselves. There's got to be a way."

"There is." Mother leaned forward and rested her head in her hand. "I've called at least eleven agencies, Nick—I didn't give them my name, of course—and they all told me the same thing. If he's dangerous to himself or others—or if I can persuade the police that he is—I can go to them and fill out emergency commitment papers."

"Well, then?"

"Do you know what happens then?" Mother dropped her hand and looked at Nick. "The police come and get him. Not an ambulance, not a medical team, but the police. If he won't go peacefully, they'll put him in a straitjacket. And they'll take him away in a squad car." Her chin trembled suddenly, and she turned away. "I can't do that to Jacob, I just can't. He would never trust me again. It would destroy whatever's left between us. . . ."

She was right, Nick knew. That would be the very last thing to try, when they had exhausted everything else.

"I keep thinking," Mother went on, "that we'll reach a point where even Jacob has to admit he needs help. Until then, there's not a thing we can do but live one day at a time."

"You think we can hold out that long, Mom? What if it's a year? Three years?"

Jacob came out of the bathroom, and the Requiem began again in the living room. Nick realized how long it had been since there had been any other music now that the students were gone. Mother used to play the piano herself in the evenings, mostly Chopin, but she clearly had no heart for it now.

"I said a day at a time," she told Nick. "Don't ask me what I'll do a year from now. I don't even know what I'll be doing next week."

NICK WAS GRATEFUL for his job. It took up time that he would otherwise have spent in the apartment. This way, there was only an hour alone with his father in the late afternoon, then study after dinner. There was also the invitation to Karen's that was coming up. Nick looked forward to it, except for his secret knowledge that Danny wouldn't be there.

It irked him the way Danny chattered on all week as though he would. All during lunch Friday, right up to the bell, he joked with Karen about bringing over his Chinese checkers. He tried to make her believe that he was a checkers champion and took it very seriously.

"I can't believe this," Karen laughed, not knowing if he was teasing. "I thought we were going to play poker."

Danny rolled his eyes in mock horror. "Never touch the stuff," he said.

Nick laughed along with the others, but when they left the cafeteria, he murmured, "You should have told her."

"I'll call her after school," Danny said.

The Saturday of Karen's invitation, Nick had to work at the deli from ten until five. When he finished unloading a truck, cleaning the windows, and scrubbing the floor in the back room, his muscles cramped when he tried to straighten up. He was more tired than he'd been the week before.

"Hang in there," Mr. Perona said. "You're doing okay."

All Nick wanted to do afterwards was sit in the tub, hot water up to his neck, feet propped high on the wall to soothe them. But he picked up Lois about seven-fifteen and walked back with her to the apartment building. As they started across the foyer, she said, "Where's your apartment, Nick?"

"That staircase," he said, pointing to the one on the right.

"Why don't we go up and say hello to your folks?"

Nick's throat seemed to go into spasm. He guided her on toward the left staircase. "Some other time," he said. "Mom wasn't feeling too well tonight."

Lois accepted it easily, but Nick knew that eventually he'd run out of excuses.

At the Zimmerman apartment Nick could tell the minute Karen answered the door that Danny had called.

"Danny can't come," she said disappointedly. "His cousin arrived this afternoon, and his mother says he has to show her around."

Nick tried to register surprise.

"Why didn't he bring her over here?" Lois asked, taking off her jacket.

"I suggested it, but he said they were all going out for dinner and a movie. Anyway," Karen added, closing the door behind them, "I'm glad *you* two could come, at least."

"Three's a party!" called out Mrs. Zimmerman gaily from the kitchen where she was stirring something chocolate.

Karen was not much good at hiding disappointment, Nick decided. She laughed and said all the right things, but in between, in the lapses of conversation, she took up that strange little buzzlike hum as though to comfort herself. It always seemed strange to Nick that sometimes the best-looking girls or guys didn't seem to know how attractive they really were and were as lonely and insecure as anyone else.

For the rest of the evening, Nick tried hard to make things go well for Karen and Lois. Tried not to think about Danny out with another girl, tried not to think about why he himself could never ask friends to the apartment across the lobby.

"How did the date go with the girl from church?" Nick asked Danny on Monday when they met at the Y to shoot baskets.

"Great!" Danny dribbled the ball around in a circle and made a long shot. "I asked Marlene to sort of keep May second free and I'd let her know later about plans." He made another toss, retrieved the

144

ball, and passed it to Nick. "Last night I called Karen and asked her to go to the dance and she said yes. So I've got one bird in hand and another in the bush. Pretty good, huh?"

Nick shook his head in disbelief. "What are you going to tell Marlene if things *don't* fall through with Karen?"

"Tell her we'll go out the next night instead. She goes to another school, so she won't know anything about our dance. I believe in insurance, buddy. This boy isn't about to lose the price of a ten dollar ticket because a girl changes her mind at the last minute. Ask Lois to go and we'll double."

"It's still seven weeks away!"

"If you don't, someone else will. A lot of the guys have dates already."

Lois, when Nick called, faked surprise. "The spring semi-formal? When is it, Nick?" As though there hadn't been posters all over school for a week.

"May second," Nick told her. "Danny's going with Karen and we can double."

"Great! Really fantastic!"

Well, *something* was going fantastic, anyway, Nick thought. At least he had friends. He had a job. A date for the dance. Dad's illness wasn't the end of the world.

He also had relatives, and when Nick came home from work one afternoon, he found Uncle Thad sitting in the living room across from Jacob.

The atmosphere was tense; the air fairly crackled with electricity. Thaddeus merely turned toward Nick, nodded soberly, and went on talking:

"Okay, Jacob, you asked me for help and I came. But you've turned down every one of my suggestions."

Nick stood rooted to the floor, looking from one to the other.

"You won't see a doctor, you won't try to get another job, you won't let me drive you to the VA hospital. . . ."

Nick tried to imagine his father calling Uncle Thad for help. It must have been in a blind panic, in a rush of fear so great that it made him desperate.

But the curled-up smile settled on Jacob's face again and he stiffened.

"I don't need your help," he said. "Forget I ever asked."

"You need it, you just don't want to admit it."

"So they've brainwashed you, too."

Nick crossed the room and went on out to the kitchen. Wasn't this where he came in? Wasn't this the same reply Jacob made to everyone?

Uncle Thad's voice grew louder, more irritated: "Now look here, Jacob, don't add *me* to your list. You don't know what you're talking about."

"That's the whole trouble," Nick's father retorted. "I know too much."

Nick started to eat some crackers, then took them

across the hall to his room and shut the door. He couldn't stand listening to it. He knew what his father would say before he said it. Certain phrases were repeated so often they seemed to come automatically from Jacob's lips: *I know too much; it was a mistake to come here; the only way Jacob Karpinski will get out of Chicago is in a box.* Nick turned on his radio and ate noisily.

By the time Mother came home at six, Thad was gone, Jacob had resumed his hunched position at the window, watching for shadows on the street below, his bravado gone, and Nick had the spaghetti sauce heating. It was as though Thad had never been there at all. Nick didn't even tell his mother. There was nothing to tell.

That evening, Grandpa Rycek called. Nick answered.

"Nick! How come we haven't heard from you folks lately?" he said. "Now you tell me, how's everything going? How's school?"

This was only to pass the time, Nick knew. First the talk about school; the questions about Jacob would come later.

"Hi, Gramps. Well . . . school's okay. And I got a job at the deli."

"The deli, huh? Not eating up all the profits, are you?"

Nick strung out the words, throwing in references to his mother every so often, saying things like "we" as though he were talking about the whole family, trying to make it sound as though he were including them all. When he ran out of things to say, he put his mother on the line.

And Jacob, his face serious and drawn, sat over a waste basket in the living room, trimming his nails —carefully, methodically—examining each one as though it would give him a clue, somehow, of what lay ahead, of what would happen next.

AT SCHOOL, Nick avoided Miss Etting's corridor, afraid that if he said any more, he would slip up somehow and she might find out. Also, he was feeling angry that there was so little anyone could do to help. *Do* something, everyone seemed to imply —Miss Etting, the priest—but no one knew what.

Nonetheless, Miss Etting found him one day in the west corridor on his way to Spanish.

"Nick," she said, reaching out and catching his sleeve. "I've been wanting to ask. . . . How's your friend's father?"

Nick stood sideways to show he was in a hurry. "Oh, about the same I guess. Haven't seen him lately."

"Did they talk with the family doctor?" Miss Etting's eyes were sincere. She really cared. Nick was sorry he was so abrupt with her.

"I don't know," he said, "but if I hear anymore, I'll let you know."

It had not been a good week. Jacob had announced on Wednesday that the Communists wouldn't let him die after all, that they wanted the pleasure of torturing him slowly themselves. His voice had an accusing tone, but this time Mother said nothing. Nick watched her grimly eating her toast, eyes on her plate, and a moment later Jacob angrily left the table, insisting that the family didn't care.

There were times Nick felt that everything his father did required an audience. Maybe this was the way to force a confrontation. If they didn't react, maybe he would take the initiative to help himself.

There were other times, however, when Jacob was so panicked that Nick could hear his shallow breathing clear across the room. Jacob was so frightened, in fact, that when he got up, the back of the chair would be damp with his perspiration. The fear was so strong, sometimes, it was like a tangible substance there in the room.

Wanda Karpinski began hiding the kitchen knives each night before she went to bed. Nick had seen her doing it, saw her wrapping them up in a dish cloth and placing them under the sacks beneath the sink. She would get them out each evening when she came home for dinner, and put them away again before she went to bed. Nick did not need to ask why.

A NEW SHIPMENT of cheese arrived at the deli, and Nick spent the afternoon unloading it, helping

Mr. Perona cut it into chunks, wrapping it, weighing it, then sticking on labels before he packed it in the huge refrigerator in the back room. After that the shelves had to be dusted, the floor swept, and some barrels hauled to the basement. Nick's body was beginning to adapt to the work, and he was glad to have something physical to do at the end of the school day. When the clock read five, he would have liked to work longer, anything to keep from going home, but Perona waved him on.

"Time you got home to your family, Nick," he said.

Outside the air was warm and Nick found himself thinking about summer against his will. He erased it from his mind. Planning for anything was a luxury he couldn't afford.

The phone started ringing when he reached the top of the stairs and he quickly let himself in the apartment and answered.

"Nick?" It was Lois. "You sound breathless."

"Just got home. Heard the phone ringing."

"I walked off with your pen after sixth period and thought maybe you were looking for it."

"Didn't even miss it," he laughed.

"Anyway, I gave it to Karen and she said she'd drop it by."

Nick felt his body tensing. "That's okay. I'll walk over and pick it up."

They talked on about the biology test, and as

soon as Nick hung up, he went back downstairs and over to the Zimmerman apartment. No one answered.

When he got back, he looked around for his father and found him lying on his bed, fingers folded tightly over his chest, eyes on the ceiling.

"You okay, Dad?"

In answer, Jacob stretched out one hand, motioning Nick to come over, and gripped his arm tightly.

Nick sat down beside him. "What's up?"

"Nick . . ." Jacob whispered, and his breath was stale-smelling and musty. He looked ill. "Tonight . . . they're coming for me tonight. I've seen the signs."

"Dad . . ." If there were a million words in the English language, Nick was thinking, there still wouldn't be the words he needed to reassure his father.

Jacob raised his head a few inches off the pillow, his neck stiff as though a board braced his back. "They're going to cut me up in little pieces. I know."

"Dad, where do you get this stuff? It sounds like a detective story."

"They're coming, Nick. I've heard."

Nick knew better than to ask what Jacob heard or how he knew. The replies never made sense. "Listen," he said. "You want me to call Uncle Thad and we'll take you over to the VA hospital? You can hide out there." He was ashamed of himself for playing on the fear, but he could think of nothing else.

151

"Thad's one of them, Nick. He doesn't want to be, but he is. They'll kill him if he doesn't play along."

If only he could drive Dad there himself, Nick thought. "Okay, then, you want me to call Mom? We can get a cab and take you over."

Jacob looked at him strangely, then got up suddenly and thrust his shirt back in his trousers. Without a word he went down the hall to the living room and opened the front closet for his jacket.

"You going somewhere, Dad? Want me to come along?"

"No. You stay here."

"I'll go," Nick said quickly, following along after him.

"No!" This time Jacob turned on him vehemently. "I said stay here!"

"Okay, okay."

Nick waited until his father was downstairs, then slipped down after him, but when he saw him head for the car, he knew it was useless to follow. He tried Karen's apartment again. Still no one there. Once a week, she'd told him, she went out to dinner with her parents. Maybe that was it.

Jacob did not come home for supper. Mother and Nick toyed with the chicken there on their plates.

"There are times," Mother said at last, carefully rationing out the words as though she were thinking

152

each syllable through before she spoke, "when I wish it was over. How*ever* it's going to end."

"So do I," said Nick.

"Oh, Nick." She dropped her head on her chest and covered her eyes with her hands. "I never thought I would say that. I never thought—when I married him—it would be like this. . . ."

"Well, it *wasn't* always."

"No. I keep trying to remember the good times."

"What kind of family were they, Mom—him and Thad? Did you ever meet his parents?"

She picked up her fork again and seemed relieved to be talking. About anything.

"Once. They came to America once, just after you were born. They wanted to see their grandson." She smiled just a little.

"What were they like?" Nick was trying to pass the time too, he knew—anything to keep his mind off the clock that said it was getting later and later.

"I never got to know them, Nick. They didn't know much English, and I didn't speak Polish. Jacob interpreted for us. They were pretty, oh, formal, I guess you'd call it. The one thing . . . the thing I remember most is that they hardly ever smiled. Or when they did, it was at you. Or at me. But not at each other. And not at Jacob. That I remember very clearly. They never smiled at Thad or Jacob."

She took a bite, paused for a moment at a noise in

the hallway, then—hearing their neighbor's door close—resumed chewing. "It seemed a rather stern household, and Jacob never enjoyed talking about what it was like, living with his parents, so I didn't ask. I just know that he and Thad had a chance to go to school in this country when they were in their late teens. Had a chance and took it. And maybe the parents never forgave them for that. Or maybe things were so bad at home that the boys felt they had to get away."

"America's about as far away as they could get," Nick mused. Then added, "I think it's lucky for Dad he found you, Mom."

Wanda gave a laugh that ended up in tears. "Lucky!" she said, and shook her head. "Yes, we sure are lucky, aren't we?"

There was a noise again in the hallway, and this time it was their own door opening. Then the sound of a package rustling, of the closet door being swung open. More rustling.

Nick got up and went into the other room. Jacob closed the closet door quickly, avoiding his eyes.

"Jacob, supper's been waiting!" Mother said, from the doorway.

Jacob sat down at the table and began eating mechanically, not even bothering to see what was before him. Nick helped his mother put their own dishes in the sink, then went back to the living room and quietly crossed to the closet. A tall, slender package that said "Sears" stood propped in one corner. Reaching in, Nick felt along the outline of the object beneath, trying to decide what it was. His hand traveled along something hard and metal, and then something wooden and wider at the bottom. He froze suddenly as the image came to mind. A rifle.

A chair scraped in the kitchen, and before Nick could stand up, his father came striding across the room.

"Get away from that!" Jacob swooped down and jerked the package out of the closet, glaring at Nick. Mrs. Karpinski came to the doorway, wondering.

"Mom, it's a gun," Nick said.

"Jacob. . . ?"

Jacob took the package over to the couch and sat down, unwrapping the paper. The dark wood stock of a rifle was exposed first, then the sights, then the barrel.

"They're coming," Jacob said to no one in particular, "and I'm going to be ready."

"Jacob, we are *not* having a gun around here," Mother said, her voice trembling with tension. "I simply won't allow it."

"The Constitution allows it," said Jacob.

A small box fell out of the package and Jacob opened it up and slipped a bullet into the chamber. There was a noise outside as the woman across the hall went to the incinerator. Jacob tensed.

Nick could hear his own pulse throbbing in his

head as he exchanged glances with his mother. The minutes ticked by. Every so often Jacob nervously lifted the rifle and examined it, then laid it back across his knees, eyes on the door, ears straining for every sound.

"Let me have the gun, Jacob," Mother said softly, holding out her hand. There was no response.

Nick imagined himself rushing his dad and trying to wrest the rifle from him. It would never work. Jacob was almost twice as heavy, strong as an elephant. Nick thought next of grabbing the box of bullets. Then they'd only have to worry about the one in the gun.

And then there was another sound outside, the soft thud of footsteps on the stairs.

Jacob lifted the rifle once more, a trace of sweat on his forehead. "I'm ready," he said again, and his hand was shaking.

Mother turned helplessly toward Nick.

The footsteps had reached the first landing and were starting up the second flight. And between footsteps there came the sound of someone humming.

Ten

NICK SPRANG for the door, flung it open, and went crashing down the stairs, colliding with Karen Zimmerman on the landing below.

His first thought was to turn his wild rush into a joke, pretend that he and Dad were horsing around —but his face muscles locked and he could not even smile.

"Nick. . . ?"

He had knocked Karen against the wall and, as a couple looked up from second floor, Nick took Karen's arm and pulled her on down the stairs with him.

"C'mon," he said, and she followed, staring at him hard.

They passed the couple on second and hurried on down to first. In the lobby, Nick stood leaning against the radiator, his heart pounding, cold terror creeping up the calves of his legs. The relief of knowing that Karen was safe was extinguished immediately when he thought of his mother alone in the apartment with Dad. He ought to go back.

"Nick, what's wrong?"

He hesitated. "A quarrel with my dad, that's all."

"Oh. I came at a bad time, didn't I?"

"It's okay."

She held out the pen. "Lois asked me to give you this. She didn't realize she'd taken it."

"Thanks." Nick slipped the pen in his pocket. "Listen, I have to go back up. I'll see you tomorrow, okay?"

"Sure."

She was watching him quizzically, and Nick was glad when he had turned the stairs at the first landing and was out of sight. As he started up the next flight to the second floor, however, he felt as though every nerve in his body were waiting for the sound of a gunshot, that every muscle had tensed, ready to plunge either forward or back.

He wondered if he shouldn't call the police instead. How much more desperate could things get than this? Just run down to Walgreens, call the emergency number, and tell them that his father had a gun.

The scenario played itself out before his eyes. Two, possibly three, squad cars would arrive, sirens going. One officer would slip up the fire escape while the others tried to divert Jacob's attention in the hall. He thought of the way the name and the address would be broadcast over the radio squawking there in the police car: *a family quarrel . . . deranged man, armed with a rifle . . . Jacob Karpinski. . . .*

And then Nick imagined the look on his father's face when he realized that he was surrounded, when all his worst fears were realized. What might he do to himself? To Mom? Nick's feet kept moving upward on the stairs, in syncopation with the beating of his heart.

It occured to him that Jacob would be listening for footsteps, wondering who was coming. He concentrated on trying to make the sound of his footsteps familiar, but who knew his own footsteps that well? At the second landing he paused, waiting, then began the trek to the third floor, whistling shakily as he came. When the apartment door came into view, his eyes scanned it quickly for the muzzle of a gun.

"Dad?" he called, "It's me. Nick."

He took another step. He had to get the rifle away from his father, had to get it out of the apartment. He reached the top of the stairs, where the door stood ajar.

"Dad?" he called again. "It's Nick."

Behind him, the neighbor's door closed softly.

Bracing himself, Nick stepped through the doorway into the Karpinski apartment. The rifle lay on the couch, the wrapping paper on the floor, and from the bathroom came the sound of his father vomiting.

Mother came quickly down the hall.

"He's so frightened he's sick," she said, her own voice shaky. She grabbed up the Sears wrapping paper and the rifle, and thrust them at Nick. "Get rid of this—take it back. Hurry."

Nick swept up the box of bullets from the coffee table and rushed back out, not even stopping to get his jacket. In the lobby, he released the clip, then checked the bottom of the sack. No receipt. Dad must have kept it in his wallet. There were several Sears stores in Chicago where Jacob could have made the purchase. Nick knew of only the one on Lawrence, however, so he set off for the el.

He sat woodenly with the rifle between his knees, the barrel sticking up out of the sack. His mind felt numb—frozen. He tried to concentrate on anything at all, but nothing seemed to stick. He focused on the biology test the next day. He forgot what chapters, what page numbers, what topics, even.

Despite the earlier warmth of the afternoon, it was cold when Nick reached the store, and he felt chilled through. He took the escalator up to sporting goods on second and waited at the counter behind a man and his young son who were purchasing a rod and reel. Nick listened to the easy banter between them, watched the smiles of the boy as he ran his finger up and down the rod. *You don't know how lucky you are*, Nick thought. Right now, the idea of being in a normal family seemed more important—and more unattainable—to Nick than he had ever imagined.

"*Yes*, sir!" the clerk said brightly, when it was Nick's turn.

"I'd like to return this rifle."

The clerk smiled. "Didn't get any big game with it, huh?"

Nick didn't answer. There was something about the clerk's cavalier attitude that irritated him. He wondered if this was the same man who had sold it to his father; if anyone, no matter how desperate, could just walk in a store and buy a gun.

The clerk opened the box of bullets and made a quick check. "One's missing," he said.

"It's in the gun."

The clerk studied him, opened the chamber, and the bullet fell out in his hand. "Receipt?"

"I don't have it. My father bought it."

"Sure he bought it from this store?"

"No," said Nick. "I'm not."

The clerk stopped smiling and clearly showed his irritation. "I've got to have a receipt," he said. "Did he charge it or pay cash?"

Forcing out the words, Nick said coldly, "My father is mentally ill and we were afraid he might shoot someone. I can't get you the receipt. This is all I have."

The clerk's eyes seemed to go from green to gray, the face to change, the jaws to stiffen.

"I'll take care of it right away," he said. The rifle and bullets were whisked down behind the counter as though to keep them from making their way back to the Karpinski apartment, and two minutes later, Nick was on his way down to the credit office for a refund while the clerk stared after him.

He walked to school the next morning beside Karen and part of him said, *Tell her*. Now that his mouth had formed the words and said them once, even to an unknown sales clerk, perhaps it wouldn't be so difficult the second time around. But the words seemed to get halfway up his throat and stop. Strange how he would rather have her believe that he and his father had quarreled—quarreled so violently that Nick had been chased from the apartment—than he would have her know the truth. Nick Karpinski, the keeper of secrets.

She didn't bring it up.

"The dance is only a couple weeks off," she told him. "I'm glad we're going with you and Lois."

"Yeah. It'll be fun."

Karen sighed. "Still seems like a lot of fuss for just one evening though, doesn't it? Mom wants to buy me a new dress, but I'm just going to wear one of my sister's."

"You're easy to please," Nick smiled.

"About *some* things," she said. "Actually, I wasn't

even sure I wanted to go, but Mother says if I don't I'll regret it all my life." She laughed. "She says that about everything, of course. If I even miss going to a movie with friends, I'll regret it all my life."

Nick laughed too, but at the same time, he was wondering if small things would ever seem so important to him again. It felt sometimes as though he were far older, that he had jumped somehow from junior high to halfway through his thirties and had missed out on all the years in between.

THE FOLLOWING EVENING, there was company for dinner.

"Jacob," Mother said cautiously, hanging up her coat in the closet as Nick watched, "I've invited Father Thomas for dinner this evening."

"I was on my way to the deli to get my supper and she rescued me," the priest said, smiling broadly, but even the width of his smile couldn't hide from Nick, or Jacob either, that this was more than a casual encounter; it was all too obvious that Mother had asked the priest for help.

Jacob glared sullenly at them both.

"How do you do, sir?" Father Thomas said, and went directly across the room, his hand outstretched. Stiffly, Jacob shook it.

The priest was a short man, several years younger than Jacob, with a bald spot on the top of his head.

Despite his height, he looked as though he might have been a wrestler at some time, and Nick felt comforted in having him there. As soon as Father Thomas shook Jacob's hand, he turned to Nick.

"I've seen you at the deli. How do they treat you? That a good place to work?"

"It's okay," Nick said. "Mr. Perona's all right." He was wondering how they were supposed to make the tuna casserole feed four people; then he saw that Mother had bought some things to round out the meal.

Father Thomas was a good conversationalist, and when Jacob didn't answer a question, he answered it himself so skillfully that he hardly lost a beat. The cole slaw went around the table, and the pumpernickel and the tuna, and the priest ate heartily, thickly buttering his bread and including Jacob in the conversation whether he contributed anything or not.

He pulled no punches, however. When Mother got up later to make the coffee, Father Thomas rested his elbows on the table and looked Jacob square in the eyes. "Wanda is worried about you, Jacob, and I'd like to do what I can. How can I help you?"

Nick, watching from across the table, wondered if Jacob would stare him down. For a full minute they studied each other's face, but it was Jacob, at last, who blinked.

164

"If I need you, Father, I'll let you know," he said sardonically.

"How can I help?" the priest said again, without malice.

"No one can help me now," Jacob retorted.

"I can if you'll let me," the priest said.

"Did *they* send you?"

"No one sent me. I came at your wife's invitation, nothing more."

For a moment Nick thought his father might give in, might talk—thought his face had lost some of its cynicism. But then Jacob merely grunted, folded his arms across his chest, and turned his face toward the window.

When Mother came back in with the coffee, Father Thomas said, "I'm leading a retreat for married couples next week—a lovely place up in Waukegan. Why don't you come for one of our three-day sessions? It would make a nice break for the two of you. I think you'd enjoy it, Jacob."

Wanda looked quickly at Jacob, but Nick knew even without thinking that the answer was no.

The cold smile played about his father's mouth. "And once you had me up there, what would happen?"

Father Thomas studied him. "What would you *like* to happen?"

"I want to live," said Jacob.

"It would be a beginning," said the priest. "You

are hardly living now, Jacob. This isn't any kind of life, shut up in here month after month with your fears."

"They want to see me punished," Jacob said.

Father Thomas shook his head. "The punishment is coming from yourself. No one else."

Jacob's smile grew wider, and Nick closed his eyes against it. He hated that smile, fought against it, refused to look at it any longer.

"The Commies," Jacob said slowly, "are very thorough in their brainwashing. They'll take any-body—priests, postmen, wives, sons—it doesn't make any difference."

Father Thomas put his hands against the edge of the table and prepared to get up. "Think about it, Jacob," he said. "If you decide to come, you and Wanda, you can attend any session you like. Come up either Monday or Thursday. No charge. I'd be pleased to see you." He stood up then. "I have counseling sessions tonight so I have to run." He shook Mother's hand. "Delightful meal, Wanda. You can tell by all I put away." Then he shook Nick's hand, but Jacob got up and went back to the bed-room, shutting the door.

Mother turned to Father Thomas. "You see. . . ?"

"Yes, I see." He shook his head sadly.

"What can we do, Father?"

"Nothing until he lets us. Unless you want to get the police in on it."

"No." Mother shook her head. "I can't," she said helplessly. "I just can't. Not unless he was threatening Nick or me."

"Then it might be too late."

"No," Mother said again. "I just can't."

Nick couldn't either. As angry as he'd been at his father, as frightened, as weary, it hadn't come to that. Not yet.

"Listen . . ." Father Thomas moved toward the door and picked up his hat from off the chair. "See if you can't get him to the retreat. Maybe, away from here, among new faces, he would get a different perspective. Maybe he would agree to hospitalization himself."

"I'll try," said Mother, but her voice was flat. "Thanks for coming."

"Call me anytime. If there's any change, let me know."

In the days that followed, Dad seemed to grow worse. Nick went to school in the morning and stood in the locker room with Danny, talking about where they would take the girls after the dance, and then he would come back home to find his father taping up the razor slots in the medicine cabinet, the electric sockets, the crack under the door. Nick would walk to school beside Karen talking of basketball scores and homework assignments, then come home after work to find his father in the shower, trying to wash off the invisible powder that he said was seeping into the apartment and eating away at his skin.

The Sunday before the dance, just as the family sat down to dinner, Jacob announced that he was being poisoned. Silently Mother reached over, slid Jacob's plate toward her side of the table and put her own plate in front of him. But even that didn't help.

"The poison won't affect *you*," Jacob said. "The Commies will see to that."

The phone rang, and before Nick could get it, his father swung around and lifted the receiver.

"Who is this?" he demanded. "Lois who?"

"It's for me, Dad," Nick said, stumbling over his chair. "Let me have it." He grabbed the phone from his father's hand.

"Nick! Who was *that*?" Lois asked.

"Dad," Nick said, without elaborating.

"Yikes! He sounded furious! What did I do, call at a bad time?"

"It's all right. How you doing?"

"Listen, I just . . . well, I thought you might want to know the color of my dress."

Nick tried to collect his thoughts, tried to think of why he would possibly want to know the color of a dress. Then he realized that the dance was on Friday and he would need to order a corsage.

"Oh, yeah! Sure! I was going to call you," he said.

"Blue and silver," she told him.

"Sounds great. Right."

He had to remember to order those flowers. Had to try on his suit coat too, see if the sleeves were too short. Had a lot to remember. Danny Beck's father was going to drive both ways, so at least he wouldn't have to worry about that.

Later that evening, there was a crisis of a different sort. Nick was sitting in the kitchen eating a bowl of ice cream when the phone rang again. He answered, spoon suspended over his dish.

"Nick, I'm in trouble!" The voice sounded muffled and far away.

Nick jerked upright and laid down his spoon.

"Danny? Where are you?"

"In the closet."

"*What?*"

"I pulled the phone in here so my folks couldn't listen."

"What's the matter? What's happened?"

"I just got back from Youth Fellowship at our church. Marlene bought a dress."

"What are you talking about?"

"For the *dance*! Somehow she found out about our semi-formal and figures I'm going to ask her this week."

"Oh, cripes!" Nick rested his forehead in his hand. "You and your birds in bushes, Danny! You'll just have to ask her out someplace real special the following night, like you said."

Danny's voice cracked. "Nick, it's a *long* dress! One of her friends told me. It's a *strapless* dress that cost a hundred dollars! Where the heck am I going to take her in a strapless dress?"

"Oh, jeez!"

"Nick, I'm a nerd."

"Don't remind me."

"I'm a jerk! A louse! What the heck am I going to do?"

"Take them both," Nick said dryly.

"Don't joke!" Danny pleaded.

"Well, you can't let Karen down."

"Tell me something I don't know." Danny was miserable. "I'm going to be sick. I'm going to get the flu and stay home."

"That's ten bucks for tickets down the drain, then. Two girls left with long dresses they can't wear."

A desperate howl came over the line.

"Maybe we can find a date for Marlene," Nick said. "I can't think of anything better. We'll ask around Monday, okay?"

Danny gave a final whimper and Nick had to smile as he hung up.

ON MONDAY, Nick stopped at the florist's beside the el and ordered white carnations with a blue and silver ribbon. He made it to the deli two minutes late, offered a quick apology to Perona, and hurried on back to the stockroom. He hoped the evening at home would be peaceful, that Jacob would keep his fears under control for this one night—just let him have some rest. But when he arrived home shortly after five, he found his father complaining of pains throughout his system. The poison was spreading, Jacob told him: every joint, every bone, had begun to ache. He refused to eat with the rest of the family, but ate only a handful of crackers from a box he just opened, a few cookies from a previously sealed package, a can of juice, a new jar of peanut butter.

He lay down after supper, insisting that the poison had spread to his brain. He was still there when Nick went to bed. Carefully, Nick rebuilt the tower of books and marbles that would alert him if Jacob came in during the night.

About midnight, he heard the books fall over, the tin box of marbles go skidding across the floor. Nick bolted up on one elbow.

"Nick, what on earth. . . ?" It was Mother's voice.

"What time is it?" he asked her, wondering if he'd slept through the alarm again.

"Just past midnight. Jacob is very upset and wants to go to the hospital. He says he'll really go this time. Will you come with us?"

Not again. Nick lay for a moment without moving, then groggily stumbled out of bed and pulled on his jeans and sweater. He slipped his sneakers on over bare feet and went into the bathroom to wash the sleep from his eyes.

In the back bedroom, Jacob's breath came short and shallow and his face was pale, the worry lines etched deep. He was carelessly throwing clothes in a suitcase, scarcely watching what he was doing. *Maybe this time it's for real*, Nick thought.

"I've got to get out of here," Jacob said again and again. "They're coming for me. They'll take me away."

"The hospital will take care of you, Jacob," Wanda said, packing his electric razor.

"I ought to be in a hospital. I know it now. I know they're coming."

"Call Father Thomas," Mother said to Nick. "Ask him to come right over."

Nick hesitated, then went to the phone in the kitchen. He did not like calling the priest at one o'clock in the morning. The phone rang and rang, and after the eighth ring, he was ready to hang up when someone answered.

"Is this Father Thomas?"

The voice at the other end was full of sleep. "He's not here."

"Do you know where I could reach him?"

"He's out of town at a retreat. Is there a message?"

The retreat. They had forgotten.

"No," Nick said. "No message." And hung up.

Back in the bedroom, Jacob was beginning to stall, and Nick felt the old panic rising in his chest.

172

"Can I help, Dad?" he asked. "Want me to carry that to the door?"

The decision of what to take and what to leave had begun to slow Jacob down, and at last Nick took his father's arm. "Come on, Dad, this is enough. If you need anything else, Mom and I will bring it to you later. Have you got your keys? Do you know the way to the VA hospital?"

"I need protection," Jacob said again. "The government has to protect me. They have to take me in, Nick. I can tell them anything they want to know. I know how the Commies operate."

"Come on, Dad," Nick said again.

"Let's take a cab, Jacob," Mother urged.

"No!" Jacob shouted the word, so Mother flung on her coat and they all went downstairs.

Holding onto his father's arm, Nick could feel it trembling, could hear his father's breathing as it came shakily through his lips.

"I'll sit in the middle this time," he said, sliding in the front seat beside Jacob, and Mother got in after him. His heart pounded fiercely. He wanted to be close enough to grab the wheel in an emergency, though he wasn't at all sure that he could.

Ten minutes out on the streets, however, the moaning and trembling and sighing began to let up, to be replaced for a time with silence. And then the complaints began. Nick closed his eyes in despair. Why did they never learn?

"Run out of my own apartment in the middle of the night," Jacob said to no one in particular. "A man without a home. A man without a country."

Nick could sense his mother's futility in the way her hands lay overturned in her lap.

"Oh, *you* can't help it," Jacob went on. "*You'll* do all right without me. The Commies will see to that." The words shot from his mouth in a shower of spit.

Nick had only a general idea of where the VA Hospital was located, somewhere west of the city, but the Pontiac had taken a turn and was going south. It began to pick up speed. Mother's hand clutched at Nick's.

"Jacob," she cried, when the car careered around a corner and the back wheels went over a curb. "Be careful!"

The Pontiac slowed for another two blocks or so, then the motor raced again. The roads were virtually deserted, and the streetlights lit an eerie emptiness, like a stage without players.

"I see through you now," Jacob snarled. "Traitors, that's what you are. Well, if I go, I'm going to take some people with me. Jacob Karpinski's not going to give up without a fight."

The car barely missed a construction site in the center of the street and went screeching up another road marked "One Way."

"Oh, Nick!" Mother was whispering.

They were going forty miles an hour in a twenty-five-mile zone. The tires squealed as they rounded another corner and headed for the loop, sideswiping a street sign. In terror, Nick wondered what would happen if he grabbed the wheel. Somehow he would have to get his father's foot off the gas at the same time. He couldn't do it; couldn't do two things at once. If Father Thomas were only here. . . .

The Pontiac suddenly slowed as it approached a red light a block away. Nick leaned forward and stared through the darkness. A patrol car from the opposite direction was stopped at the light. Slowly, carefully, Jacob brought the Pontiac to a polite stop. The squad car had its blinker flashing, ready to make a left turn. The Pontiac waited. Nick waited. One second; two seconds. . . . Nick's heart thumped loudly in his chest. Then suddenly he reached over, across his father's arm, pressed his hand down on the horn, and held it there.

Eleven

A TWO-TONED BLAST fractured the early morning stillness, separating all that had gone before from what would be. In those four or five seconds, Nick knew beyond doubt that it also separated him from his father.

"Stop it!" Jacob hissed, and tried to knock Nick's hand away, but Nick hung on. When he released it at last, Jacob swore.

Across the intersection, the squad car's blinker cut off, and instead of turning, the car moved slowly toward them through the red light. It passed, made a wide U-turn on the street, and pulled up behind them. Jacob swore again, his eyes on the rearview mirror. Mother sat with her head turned away.

Nick listened as a door behind them slammed, then footsteps sounded alongside the car. A policeman looked in the side window. In the glow from the streetlights overhead, Nick could see the officer's eyes scan their faces, then the seat, their hands. Jacob did not move. The policeman tapped on the window, and only then did Jacob roll it down.

"Good morning," the officer said. "You folks having some trouble?"

"Yes," Nick told him. "My dad's sick, and needs to get to the hospital."

The policeman looked at Jacob, then at Mother, then back to Jacob again. "You're sick, sir?"

"I am not sick," Jacob replied icily.

Please don't leave, Nick thought, trying to communicate with the policeman through his eyes. The officer straightened up and must have signaled to his partner, Nick thought, because a second door slammed and there were more footsteps.

"What seems to be the trouble?" the second officer asked.

"Well, we've got a boy here who says his dad is sick and the man says he's not."

The second officer looked into the car, smiling the official smile. "Well, son, I don't see that it's any emergency," he said to Nick.

They were going to leave, Nick could tell. He could not let that happen.

"My dad's mentally ill, and we're trying to get him to the Veteran's Hospital," he said. "Please help us."

"I am *not* going to the hospital," Jacob said.

The second officer rested his hands on the window and looked at Mother. "You the wife, ma'am?"

She turned toward him. "Yes."

"What's the story here?"

"Mom," Nick told her. "You've got to tell them."

Mother nodded. "Yes," she said without expression. "He's sick, and we need help."

Jacob neither spoke nor moved. Nick could tell, however, by the way Jacob gripped the wheel, that he was furious. Somehow, that no longer seemed to matter.

The policemen were conferring with each other in low tones, and then the first one said, "Tell you what, why don't you folks follow us back to the station, and we'll sit down with a cup of coffee and talk it over. Okay?"

Jacob did not answer.

No! thought Nick. *He won't do it! One of you drive us there*. But even as he thought it, he realized that they could not. Unless they had seen his Dad driving recklessly, they had to assume he was innocent unless proved guilty; sane, unless proved otherwise.

"Okay, sir?" the officer asked again. "Just follow us in."

They went back to their car.

"Judas Iscariot," Jacob said, looking neither at Nick nor Mother. "Sold down the river."

"Jacob, it's the only way," Mother said, and now she was weeping. "We had to do it."

Jacob swore again, and then, as the squad car pulled slowly alongside them, Jacob started the engine with a jolt and followed the policemen down the street. Any minute Nick expected the Pontiac to pull away, make a turn, tires squealing, and go careering toward the Outer Drive. But it didn't. Five minutes later, they pulled into the station.

It was a small concrete building with a few folding chairs along the bank of windows and a high desk that served as a barrier between the waiting area and the holding cells in back. The first officer spoke quietly to the desk sergeant and went on to the coffee machine in one corner, returning with cups for Mother and Jacob. Nick's father refused the coffee with a disdainful smile.

The officers arranged some chairs beside the desk for a conference, but Jacob refused to take part, pacing the length of the room nervously as someone bellowed out a long string of profanities from one of the cells.

The desk sergeant smiled pleasantly at Jacob. "Just drunks," he said. "We'll let them go when they're sober."

Jacob did not return the smile.

Nick and his mother sat down.

"How long have you suspected that he's mentally

ill?" the desk sergeant asked Mother, after taking
their name and address.

"Not more than a few months," Mrs. Karpinski
answered.

The officer wrote it down and waited, but Mother
—afraid of seeming disloyal, perhaps—did not
elaborate. Nick squirmed restlessly.

"Is Mr. Karpinski employed?"

"Not at the moment."

"Can you tell us something about the way he's
been acting?" The officer paused while Jacob passed
by the desk, then went on: "Has he hurt you?
Threatened you?"

"Oh, no. He'd never do that," said Mother.

"What, then?"

"He just . . . he paces like this . . . he doesn't go
out. He thinks that people are trying to kill him."

The sergeant's pen scratched across the paper.

"Judas Iscariot," Jacob muttered again, as he
came by the second time.

"Tell them everything!" Nick said frantically,
nudging his mother. "How you hid the knives. How
he tried to kill himself."

But the desk sergeant signaled Jacob over. "Mr.
Karpinski," he said, "the police aren't in any position to judge whether or not you are ill, so we're
going to have to detain you until eight o'clock when
the commissioner comes in. He'll see you first thing."

Jacob's face took on a look of alarm.

"We have to stay here all night?" he said warily, eyes darting toward the door.

"Well, sir, your wife and son can go home if they like, but we're going to have to give you a bunk back here. It's just until eight o'clock."

Mrs. Karpinski blanched.

"You're putting me in jail," Jacob said, and his voice shook.

"We're just giving you a bunk, Mr. Karpinski. We're not arresting you, just detaining you. You'll see the commissioner as soon as he comes in."

Jacab drew back. "No. You can't do this."

Mother sucked in her breath.

"Come on, now," the desk sergeant said. "We're not trying to make trouble for anybody. If the commissioner says we can release you, we'll let you go."

"Wanda!" Jacob called loudly, as the two officers escorted him back behind the desk. "Wanda!"

Nick looked away, fingers holding tightly to the edge of the folding chair, not wanting to hear, to see.

"I won't go in there!" Jacob yelled as a metal door squeaked open. "Wanda! They're not the police! You've got to stop them!"

"He's a real live one, all right," the desk sergeant murmured.

"Wanda!" Jacob bellowed again.

"Ah, pipe down," came another voice from the cell.

"Wanda! Nick! Don't let them do it!"

"Dad, you'll be all right. I promise," Nick called,

but Mother got up, her lips trembling, and went outside. She sat down on the steps, her head in her lap, crying. Nick felt he could not move. He sat frozen to his chair halfway between his mother, outside, and his father, back in the cell. The clock on the wall behind the coffee machine read two a.m.

AT THREE-THIRTY, Jacob announced he was ready to go to the hospital.

"What do you think?" one of the officers asked the desk sergeant.

"Save us a lot of trouble in the morning," the sergeant said.

Nick waited, suspended in time. For five months he had been waiting for something to happen, and always, at the last minute, the decision went unmade. He looked toward the door where his mother still sat on the steps beyond. *It's spring out*, Nick thought, *and she doesn't even know it*. She was suspended, too. And then he realized that the police might let his father go.

"Please don't let him drive," Nick told the desk sergeant. "He'll change his mind again, just like he did last night."

"Can your mother take him?"

"She doesn't drive."

"I'll have one of the men go with you, then." The desk sergeant nodded to an officer, and he went back to the cell to get Jacob.

"Good riddance!" one of the drunks called out as Nick's father left.

Jacob drove, an officer beside him in the front seat, while Nick and his mother sat in back. In the light from an occasional car that passed them, Nick could see the dark shadow of his father's beard beginning on the side of his face, the disheveled look of his hair. Five months ago, Nick would not have believed that this was happening, but nothing surprised him now. It was the way he survived. He glanced toward his mother. She rested her head on the back of the seat, eyes closed, lips pressed tightly together.

"The only question," Jacob was saying from up front, "is where the butchery will take place—the hospital or the jail. In the hospital, at least, they'll drug me first. At least it will be painless."

"Take it easy," said the policeman.

"Dead is dead," Jacob replied.

They drove on in silence, the officer with one arm over the back of the seat. Nick wondered what he would say about his father later, what policemen talked about around the coffee machine.

As the Pontiac pulled up the drive of the hospital, Jacob said: "If they say that I'm sane, you have to let me go."

"That's right," said the policeman. "If they say you can go, it's fine with me."

Nick straightened up and his eyes met Mother's. *They couldn't let him go.* The thought pressed inside his head. *How could he make the doctors under-stand? If, after all of this, the hospital wouldn't keep him, what was there left to do?* As he walked inside, his mother leaned against his arm, and at one point seemed to totter.

"You okay, Mom?" Nick asked.

She simply looked at him without smiling.

A nurse at the admitting desk came forward when she saw the policeman.

"We have a man here whose family thinks he ought to be hospitalized," the officer said. "I'll be in the waiting room if you need me."

The nurse turned to Mother. "What seems to be the problem?"

But it was Jacob who answered: "The problem is that my wife and son want me committed, and I have no intention of staying."

"Well," said the nurse, "we'll let a doctor decide that then. Would you come with me, sir, and I'll see who's on call this morning."

Jacob hesitated, then followed the nurse down the hall to an examining room.

"Nick," said his mother, sitting down beside him, "what are we going to do if they don't take him?"

"Let's wait and see, Mom."

"He's so frightened."

"So are we," Nick reminded. He was thinking how calm and logical his father seemed now, perfectly in control. It was their word against Dad's.

How could the doctors commit him? What evidence would they have?

The nurse came back for Nick and his mother and placed them in the examining room next to Jacob's. There were already voices in the neighboring room. Someone had come in and was talking to Nick's father. The voices rose and fell. Soft, polite voices. Fifteen minutes passed. Twenty. Nick felt the pressure building inside himself. Then, finally, the sound of footsteps, of a door opening, a door closing. Then the door to their own room opened and two doctors came in.

The older doctor put out his hand. "Mrs. Karpinski, I'm Dr. Rothman. This is Dr. Flanders." He sat down while the younger doctor leaned against the wall, arms folded over his chest. "I've just seen your husband and wonder what you can tell me about his problem. He obviously does not want to be admitted."

"You've got to keep him here!" Nick insisted. "Mom can't go through this anymore. She can't!" Then, realizing he had spoken out of turn, Nick stopped and drew in his breath, trying to get control of himself. His heart beat so violently he was sure that the doctors could hear it. He knew what his father had probably told them; that it was Nick and his mother who were sick; Nick and his mother who had the delusions—who wanted him put away.

"Jacob's not been well since December," Wanda

said and her voice was void of emotion, weighted down with fatigue.

"In what way has he not been well?"

"He thinks that someone's after him—the Communists. He left his job—left two jobs. Now he thinks that I'm poisoning him. He doesn't sleep. . . . *We* don't sleep."

Nick listened to her answer in a monotone.

"Has he ever tried to hurt you?"

"No."

The doctor looked at Nick. "Or you?"

The same questions, the same answers. . . .

"No, but he's tried to kill himself," Nick said, and described the scene in the snow.

The doctor wrote something down, but said nothing. They'd let Dad go, Nick knew. Jacob just didn't seem that sick. They would say that unless things took a turn for the worse, the family could obviously get by.

"He bought a gun," Nick said, his words coming faster now, "and he aimed it at the door when he heard someone coming. He says he's going to protect himself, and if he dies, he'll take a few with him. He was driving all over the road tonight, and he could have killed someone." Nick stopped for breath. The doctors studied him intently and Nick took courage: "We're trying to tell you before it's too late; no one wants to do anything until it happens."

Dr. Rothman sat tapping his fingers against his

186

knee. "There's a problem here, you see. As far as we can tell, this isn't a service-related illness, and we don't generally admit patients whose problems have nothing to do with their term in the military. It's particularly difficult in a psychiatric situation, when someone presents himself as rational and reasonable as Mr. Karpinski seems to be."

"But . . ."

The doctor interrupted. "I don't doubt that you are telling me the truth as far as you see the problem. But there can be difficulties when a patient doesn't want to come voluntarily—when it's only the family making the complaint. Is there anyone else, outside of relatives, who could support some of the things you've told us? Have any neighbors or friends witnessed his behavior?"

The answer was no, Nick knew. As tightly as a key fits in a lock, he and his mother had kept the problem to themselves.

"Have you even *talked* with anyone else about it?"

Only Uncle Thad, Nick was thinking, who was a relative, and Father Thomas, who was out of town. In all her phone calls to different agencies, Mother had never given her name. All the secrets, the excuses, the distractions had served only to bring him and his mother to this place, where there was no one they could call upon to help.

A wave of panic swept over Nick, as though he were going down for the third time, and for a moment he felt the same lightheadedness he had felt that day in gym. And suddenly he remembered.

"Yes," he said. "There's someone else you could talk to. Could I use a phone, please?"

"Go right out to the desk," the doctor instructed.

A hall had never looked so long, a corridor so empty, a telephone so frightening. Telling Uncle Thad was difficult enough. Knowing that Father Thomas knew was even more embarrassing. But this went far beyond relatives, far beyond the priest. Now it was Nick's world that the secret was invading, and it was the only chance he had left.

Shakily, he reached in his wallet and took out the little card behind his student ID. The clock on the opposite wall read four forty-five.

The phone rang and rang and with each successive ring, Nick fought against the impulse to hang up.

Then there was the sound of the receiver being lifted and a sleepy, puzzled voice said, "Hello?"

"Miss Etting?"

"Yes. . . ?"

"It's Nick Karpinski. I'm really sorry to be calling you at this hour. I know it's early."

"Nick? What is it?"

"Miss Etting . . . that friend I told you about . . . it's me."

* * *

SHE CAME in jeans and a sweater, without make-up, old sneakers on her feet. Nick watched her disappear into the conference room with the two psychiatrists.

"How can she help, Nick? What does she know?" Mother asked. And he told her.

"All this time," Mother said at last, "I thought it would be easier on Jacob—on us—if no one knew. That it would spare my pride, perhaps. It is so much more difficult to pretend . . ."

Outside, the black sky showed faint traces of gray and streaks of dusty pink. Over and over again, Nick relived the incident in the Pontiac when he had signaled the police car, the way his father swore, the look on Jacob's face when the police led him off to the holding cell. How his father must hate him now. . . .

It was some time before Dr. Rothman came out again and spoke to Mrs. Karpinski.

"We've decided to admit your husband, and Dr. Flanders and I will both sign the commitment papers. I'll call the nursing station about a bed. You're tired, I know, and I'll arrange an appointment with you later this week. We'll talk some more then."

Nick's shoulders slumped. His arms, his legs, the whole of his body seemed limp with relief. The relief of seeing someone else in charge; of knowing that Jacob was now the responsibility of the hospital, the doctors. Relief and guilt. Mother went over to the admissions desk and signed some forms.

Far down the corridor, Nick saw the door to his father's room open, and Jacob came out, accompanied by the younger doctor. They started toward the elevator at the end of the hall, but for just a moment, Jacob looked back. Stopped and looked at Nick. Nick's eyes and throat burned. He bolted from his chair in the waiting room and stepped outside. Standing alone on the steps, he cried silently, his face knotted up, fists doubled.

When the tears had subsided at last, he heard the door open behind him and turned to see Miss Etting, buttoning her sweater. He was embarrassed. For his father's sake; for his own.

"We'll both sleep better now," she said simply, holding her hand out to test for rain.

"He's so angry with me," was all Nick said.

She fished in her purse for her car keys. "Sometimes the choice isn't between what's bad and good; those are the easy ones. Sometimes you have to decide which of two unhappy possibilities will be best. Those are the hard choices, Nick, but you did it."

The police officer drove Nick and his mother home in the Pontiac, parked it out back, then called for another squad car and went on to the station.

Nick slept his first undisturbed sleep of the last several months. Once or twice he was conscious of the shouts of school children, or a siren, or the clanking of the garbage truck on the street outside. But within moments sleep had swallowed him up once more. Someone else was watching Jacob. No more worries about Dad roaming the apartment at night. No more hiding the knives. No more towers of books behind the door. Nick slept on.

A telephone ringing somewhere wove itself in and out of a dream, and then Nick knew it was no dream. His first thought was that Dad had somehow eluded the nurses and left the ward. He rolled out of bed and staggered toward the kitchen just as his mother came out of her bedroom.

"Hello?"

"This Nick Karpinski?" came a man's voice.

"Yes."

"It's three forty-five, Nick. You going to get yourself down here?"

Mr. Perona!

"I'm sorry," Nick said hastily. "I . . . I overslept. I'll be right in."

"Overslept? It's afternoon, Nick."

"I know. I'll be there in ten minutes."

Grabbing his clothes, Nick charged into the bathroom. "My job!" he said. "I forgot."

"Oh, Nick!"

Mother had a roll waiting for him when he came out of the shower and Nick wolfed it down as he ran

191

toward the street. A half-dozen excuses swam in his head. He was sick all night; his mother was sick; a relative had gone to the hospital. . . .

Perona glared at him when he came in and followed Nick into the back room.

"I can't have this, Karpinski," he said. "I told you I needed someone reliable."

"I will be, Mr. Perona," Nick said, and forced himself to look at the man, not to turn away. "Last night we had to take my dad to the hospital and I didn't get to bed until about seven this morning. I should have set my alarm, but I didn't think I'd sleep so long."

Mr. Perona's frown gave way to polite concern and his voice softened. "I'm sorry to hear that. Not serious, I hope."

This was a dress rehearsal for what would come later, Nick knew. Forcing the words out, one by one, keeping none of them back, Nick answered, "He's mentally ill. I guess I should have told you. We've known for a couple of months."

Twelve

TELLING PERONA, of course, was the easy part, and Nick's boss couldn't have been more decent about it.

"Listen," he had said, "if you need any time off to visit him, just let me know."

But Perona and Miss Etting and Father Thomas and Uncle Thad, though part of Nick's world, were not the part that worried him most. He left for school early Wednesday morning to clear his absence with the office. He had rehearsed what he would say and how he would say it, but the words never came easily.

None of his friends had called him after he got off work the day before. When you were absent from school, people generally let you alone for a day. Nick almost wished that someone *had* called. It might be easier to tell Danny and let him tell the others.

Amazing, though, what a long sleep could do. Mother had looked as good that morning as Nick had seen her for a long time. Sad, but relieved. She even ate a second piece of toast with her grapefruit and appeared, to Nick, to be awaking at last from a long, long sleep.

"I'm going to call Mama today," she told Nick as he'd gone out the door. "I'm going to invite them both down here this Sunday." And then she had fixed her gray eyes on Nick and said, "We're not going to hide anything anymore. Looking back, I wonder why we ever did. It seems as natural now to talk about it as it did then to hold it in."

Maybe. Nick did not feel obliged to tell the school secretary the details. Mother's note merely said that there had been illness in the family and Nick had been needed at home. It wasn't until noon, when he faced Danny and the girls in the cafeteria, that Nick knew he could delay it no longer.

"Boy, did you ever pick a good day to be sick!" Lois said, setting her tray down next to him. "State-wide exams yesterday—four hours worth! How you feeling?"

"It wasn't me, it was Dad," Nick said simply. "We had to take him to the hospital."

"The hospital?" The others stopped eating.

"Is it serious?" asked Danny.

Nick picked up a potato chip, then laid it back down. "Yeah, it's pretty serious," he said. "Dad's been mentally ill for a couple of months, but it wasn't till Monday night we were able to get him to a hospital."

The thing about silence, he thought later, remembering, was that it just hung there, like a question mark. But with those few words, the hardest thing in the world became the easiest. The excusing and protecting of the past five months had been infinitely worse.

"My gosh," Karen said finally. "I'm really sorry, Nick. We had no idea."

"Well, we're hoping now he'll get some help," Nick told them. He wanted to change the subject, but they were curious. It was better that they asked him questions to his face, Nick decided, than talked behind his back.

"How did you *know* he was mentally ill?" Danny said. "I mean, is it okay to ask?"

Nick opened his milk carton. "Last December, he started acting suspicious of people . . . of everybody, almost. We thought at first, when he left his job, that maybe it was something that happened at work. Now we know how sick he really was."

Lois suddenly stopped eating and put her hands to her face. "That was *him* who answered last Sunday when I called!" She turned to Karen and said dramatically, "He sounded positively ferocious! My God, I'll bet he was even suspicious of me!"

Nick took a bite of sandwich, eyes on his tray.

The conversation turned to other things, but every

so often, there was another question about Nick's father. It was both an ordeal and a relief, and Nick was grateful when the bell rang at last.

As they were leaving the cafeteria, Danny said to him, "You know, I'm glad you told us, Nick. You didn't think it would change things between us, did you?"

"I didn't think," said Nick, smiling. "But I know better now." Then, out in the hall, he whispered, "What's happening with you?"

Danny rolled his eyes. "Some guy's going to let me know in a day or two if his brother will take Marlene. I won't live through this, Nick. I won't!" Then he stopped. "Yes, I will," he said. "After what you've been through, my problem isn't such a big deal, is it?"

"Oh, I don't know." Nick laughed.

All day he had thought he was feeling better. It wasn't until he started home from work and realized Dad wouldn't be there that he knew he was numb. There hadn't been time yet to feel much more. For the past few months, his one goal—his and Mom's —was to get Dad in the hospital. Now that Jacob was there, the real fear came forward: Would Dad ever get well?

Walking through the silent rooms of the apartment, his eye picked up remnants of the Karpinski family before the sickness. One of Dad's Adidas sneakers, overturned there beneath the bed, reminded him of the time they had walked down to the lake together and climbed around on the rocks. They had gone for miles that afternoon it seemed, and never wanted to stop. Just one of the few spontaneous things that they never did again, but for that one afternoon, it was perfect. In Nick's own room, on the shelf above his desk, sat the book on scientific discoveries of the twentieth century. One night, talking at the supper table about Nick's career plans, Nick had simply mentioned that he might want to work in a lab. And the next day Dad had gone out and bought this book for him.

Nick turned away and swallowed, fighting against the sadness that was welling up, wanting the numbness to go on a while longer. It was a different kind of sadness now—not for the Jacob Karpinski who had driven recklessly around Chicago two nights before, but for the father he used to be. And Mother felt it too. That evening, when she unthinkingly started to wrap the knives and hide them, she stopped suddenly and began to cry. Without asking, Nick knew that even the Jacob Karpinski who had caused her such grief since December had left an empty place in her life.

On Thursday, Nick attended his first two classes, then spent the rest of the day in the guidance office taking the statewide exams. He finished before the last class was over, and the counselor told him he could go home. He put in his time at the deli, then went home and tried on his suit coat to check the sleeves. Maybe a quarter of an inch short, but it would do for the dance.

He went to his room later to study. Still had a lab experiment to do for Cranston over the lunch hour Friday, and a Spanish quiz to make up.

"Nick," his mother called, when the phone rang about eight. "For you."

It was Lois. Even her "Hi, Nick," sounded different.

"Is everything okay, Nick? When I didn't see you after second period, I wondered."

"Had to make up the state exams, that's all."

"Oh. Have you heard anymore about your dad? I mean, will he recover?"

"We don't know yet," Nick told her.

There was an awkward pause, and then Lois spoke with a rush: "Look, Nick, I really hope you won't take this the wrong way, but I was thinking—with your father sick and everything—maybe you really don't feel like going to the dance."

"I'm okay, Lois," he said, wondering.

"I mean, I know you must be worried to death, and I . . . well, if I was in your place, I don't think I'd feel like going *anywhere*, but I just wanted to say that if you didn't feel like going, it's really all right. I mean, you know Chuck Peters—from biology? Well, he asked me after you did, and he

still doesn't have a date, and I just thought maybe
. . . well, since Karen's not going—"

Nick's head spun. "What? Why not?"

"I don't know. I think she and Danny had an argument. But I just thought, now that Karen isn't going, and with you so worried and all, you might like to have Chuck take me."

The message came through loud and clear. It was probably all over school by now. Nick Karpinski's dad was a psycho. Lois didn't want to be seen with him.

Nick's voice sounded flat. "Maybe you're right," he said. "I guess I'd be sort of a wet blanket."

She was relieved and sympathetic at the same time and went on talking, much too fast: "With you and your mother so upset and everything, I just knew—"

"Thanks for calling, Lois. Have a good time. Okay?"

Mother was looking at him from the doorway. "Was that—?"

"Yeah. It was Lois. She's going to the dance with someone else."

"Oh, Nick! I'm so sorry! How can she possibly—?"

"She thinks she's doing me a favor, Mom. She says since I'm all upset over Dad—"

"But what right has she—?"

"Look, Mom, I'll get over it. Okay?" His voice

was sharp, but he hadn't meant it to be. There was never an end to problems, it seemed. No sooner was one squared away than he had a couple more to worry about.

HE DIDN'T see Karen at school on Friday and didn't know if she was there or not. He had the biology experiment to do over the lunch hour and the quiz to take in Spanish. He ran into Danny between classes, however, and stopped him there by the drinking fountain.

"Danny, what's with you and Karen?"

Danny looked chagrined and his face reddened. "Jeez, Nick, you won't believe this, but someone told Karen about Marlene and her hundred-dollar dress. Karen called me Wednesday night and said she didn't want to go, that I should take Marlene. This is the biggest mess I've ever made of things in my entire life, and if I get through this, I'm going to be a monk or something. But meantime, we'll pick you up same as before, Marlene and I."

"Lois cancelled out."

Danny stared. "*What*?"

"She's going with Chuck Peters."

"I can't believe this!" Danny clutched his head. "I just don't *believe* it!"

"Call Chuck and work out the details," Nick told him. "You can still double."

Danny grabbed Nick's arm. "Listen, Nick. I'm a

jerk, I know, and I'll probably louse up with Marlene and I'll deserve it. But *we're* still friends, aren't we?"

Nick had to laugh. "Yes," he said. "We're still friends. Call me tomorrow and tell me if you survived."

Stopping by Miss Etting's office after fifth period, Nick found her taking a girl's temperature, so he just stuck his head in the door.

"Thanks," he said.

She studied him a moment, then grinned. "That's the first wide-open smile I've seen on your face in a long time, Nick. A few nights of sleep must have helped."

"So did you," said Nick. "I appreciate it. I really mean that."

He hoped he might see Karen after school, but she wasn't around so he walked home slowly, enjoying—actually *enjoying*—the early May breeze, soft as a feather, that blew in from the lake. After work, he set the table for supper, but at five-forty the phone rang. It was the woman from the flower shop.

"Is this Nick Karpinski?" she said. "I have a corsage here that you ordered for this evening. I thought you should know that we close in twenty minutes."

Lois's flowers. He'd forgotten.

"Okay, I'll be over," he said, and went out.

It was a wasted trip, but Nick didn't have the nerve to tell the woman the date was off. On the way back, when he entered the lobby, he saw Karen standing by the door to the park.

"Karen?" He started toward her.

"I thought you'd be getting dressed," she said.

He glanced down at himself in mock embarrassment. "What did I forget? My trousers?"

She laughed a little. "I mean, for the dance."

"Oh! The dance!" said Nick. "Well, as it turns out, I'm not going."

She looked puzzled. "Why not?"

"Lois is going with Chuck Peters."

Karen stared unbelieving. "Oh, Nick! It's because of me, isn't it? Because I'm not going."

"No. It's because of Dad."

"I'm so sorry."

"Don't be. I've had enough of sorry for a while. Where you going?"

"Out to dinner with my folks. Dad's bringing the car around and Mom went back for a sweater. She's terrified I'm going to die of a broken heart or something, so she insisted we go out to dinner."

"Are you?"

"What?"

"Going to die of a broken heart?"

She smiled. "Not over Danny Beck, anyway. But you can always cure a broken heart by eating out. Or didn't you know?"

Nick laughed. "I didn't know."

"Mom says that any girl who breaks a date two

nights before a big dance will never be asked out again."

"I wouldn't bet on it," Nick told her. "Here. How would you like some white carnations with a blue and silver ribbon?"

Karen laughed as she lifted the lid and picked the flowers up. "What am I supposed to do with these?"

"Show them to your mother and tell her there's still hope," Nick said, and then, hearing Mrs. Zimmerman on the stairs, he added, "See you around," and went on back to the apartment.

ON SATURDAY, Nick took the afternoon off work to go with his mother to visit Jacob. They had an appointment with Dr. Rothman and a social worker afterwards. Without the use of the car, it meant a long trip on the el, then a bus transfer.

The hospital was a huge cluster of red brick buildings, some connected by brick tunnels, and each building had a number. Visitors surged up the main drive, little groups breaking off here and there heading for different buildings until finally there was only a small cluster of relatives left, destined for Building 51. Nick noticed what an untalkative bunch they were, the ones who were left. Had they all kept their worries in, like he and his mother? Had they all been ashamed to tell anyone else until they had to?

Building 51 had heavy metal screens on the windows. Nick hoped his mother wouldn't notice, but she did.

"Like cages," she said, as if to herself.

They did not go up on the ward, however. Visitors were required to give their names at the desk and the name of the patient they wished to see, and then they sat on a row of hard chairs in a recreation room and waited, gifts of magazines and candy on their laps.

An elevator door clanked somewhere out in the corridor. Nick leaned forward, searching for Jacob, as the patients were brought in wearing their ghastly green army pajamas with legs that were either too long or too short. The attendants sat down by the door and prepared to look bored.

The men came skulking, unsmiling, hands hanging loosely at their sides, eyes averted, like prisoners of war. Once in the room, the relatives greeted them in maddeningly cheerful voices, telling them again and again how marvelous they looked. *Lies*, Nick thought. *All lies*.

The green pajamas did not look good on Jacob. He was too tall, and the shoulders of the shirt were too narrow. Nick tried not to look at Jacob's trousers, which only reached the ankles, but his eyes, in their perversity, returned again and again.

"Well, here I am," Jacob said, standing before them, "with all the loonies."

Nick could not help smiling at the joke, regretted

it instantly, then wondered why he had to go on being so careful. Was it better to hide his feelings, or to treat his father as he always had, whether Jacob liked it or not?

He decided on the smile. "What the best-dressed man is wearing," he quipped.

Surprisingly, Jacob did not seem angry.

"How are you, darling?" Mother said, and hugged him. He took her hand and they sat down along the wall, Nick on the other side of his father.

Nick knew it was useless to think in terms of "better" or "worse" or even "no change." Dad didn't seem as frightened, that was certain, yet just as certain, Nick knew, there was no guarantee that even this peace would last.

Jacob was not accusing, however. He did not repeat his charges against them and seemed almost relieved that a decision had been made, that he did not have to decide anything himself, and that he had been in the hospital since Tuesday and was still alive. He kept tight hold of Mother's hand, Nick noticed, and when she gave him his favorite bar of Hershey's dark chocolate, he held it gratefully on his lap and did not ask if it were poisoned.

"Has Thad been out to see you?" Mother asked, but Jacob shook his head.

"He called," Jacob told them. "He said he would come by when he had the chance." He smiled wryly. "Thad's afraid it's catching, you know. We always saw ourselves in each other, and sometimes didn't like what we saw."

It was a strange admission from his father, Nick thought. Dad sounded more rational than he'd seemed in a long time. It was probably the medication, but Nick was encouraged.

"How's the food here, Dad?"

"Just like in the service," Jacob answered. "Lots of dried beef on toast. The army owns a ton of it."

"You tell me what you want me to bring next time and I will. Anything at all," Wanda told him.

Jacob put his arm around her shoulder and then, awkwardly holding the Hershey bar, put his other arm around Nick. "You'll be coming again?"

"Of *course* we'll come again, Jacob! At least twice a week."

"You promise? You won't let them ship me off."

"To where, Jacob! Of course we won't."

What seemed like improvement, Nick realized, was only fear in a different disguise. Before the hour was up, Jacob was looking furtively about him once more, at another patient whom he said had it in for him, and made them promise still again that they would return, that they would not let the doctors operate on his brain. But when the attendants announced that visiting hours were over, Jacob dutifully got up with the rest and took his place in line, turning only once to wave goodbye. When the elevator door clanked behind them, Mother drew back against the wall and cried.

"He's not the same man, Nick," she wept. "He's like a frightened little boy."

"He wasn't the same before either, Mom—the way he was at home."

"I know. I know. I just want to get the crying out of the way before I see Dr. Rothman."

They took turns, one seeing the doctor while the other talked with the social worker. Miss Corley was nice enough, but it was Dr. Rothman whom Nick wanted to see—the doctor who could answer the questions that had to be asked.

"I'm wondering whether my dad will get well." That was the first question, and it slipped from Nick's lips before he even sat down.

Dr. Rothman wasted no words. "I'd like to tell you that he will, Nick. With medication, he'll be better than he is now, but at this point, that's all I can promise. I know you wish I could promise more."

Nick tried to sort out the words, looking for some kind of encouragement, but it wasn't there. When he spoke again, he was embarrassed to discover that his chin trembled. The words came shakily: "Will he ever be able to go back to work?"

"I wish I could promise," the doctor said again.

The answer throbbed inside Nick's ears. He wanted to push it away, to go back to a time of not knowing, however painful it had been before. But the words were out, surrounding him there in the room. He sat with his face turned away, tongue thrust hard into one cheek.

When he could trust himself to speak, Nick said, "He was all right before." It was as though he could argue the doctor out of it—as though, if he tried hard enough, he could change things somehow.

"Sometimes people keep problems hidden a long, long time, even things like schizophrenia," the doctor said. He toyed with a paperclip on his desk, then leaned back, bending it between his fingers. "Perhaps, in all the changing of jobs that your father has done over the years, he was trying to work out worries he didn't talk about to you. It's really hard to say."

"But how did he get it? Is it inherited?" Nick knew, once the words were out, that he was asking about himself as well. Dr. Rothman seemed to know it too.

"We're learning more all the time," he said. "There are a number of things to be considered, including body chemistry." And then, looking directly at Nick, he smiled just a little. "But I would be very surprised if the same thing happened to you. If you're worried about that, Nick, the chances are very good that it won't."

It didn't seem to make any difference whether the answers were reassuring or not; tears formed in

Nick's eyes anyway, and he swallowed again and again.

"It seems to me," Dr. Rothman went on quietly, "that you've shown a remarkable degree of mental health—the way you've handled the stress so far, I mean—the persuasive way you argued for your dad's admission. You faced up to the problem and tried to find a solution, you didn't just go under. It's time to get on with your own lives, now—you and your mother—knowing that we'll do everything we can for your dad. If you have any questions along the line, you can call me here. I want you to know that."

Neither Nick nor his mother spoke when they met again in the hall. Mother stopped in the women's room, and Nick went on outside to wait, his eyes wet. He knew that even though he would be back, again and again, he was saying a kind of goodbye, not to Jacob himself, but to the Dad he had wanted him to be. And while he still hoped and believed what Dr. Rothman said about how they were learning more all the time, he knew he had to prepare himself for a future that might not include Jacob at all.

He looked up at the high windows of the brick building. Somewhere up there Dad was probably staring out at the sky, through the heavy mesh screen that kept him in. Did he ever, Nick wondered—in the middle of the night, perhaps—ask himself if he might have been wrong, and the world outside was more friendly than he had imagined?

Or would he go on feeling, for the rest of his life, that it was his family who could not understand, who did not care? It was this thought that was so intolerable to Nick.

They stood at the bus stop, Nick and his mother, facing in different directions. Nick knew they would feel better if they could only talk, but for a while his own pain was too sharp, and he stood hunched over.

It was Mother finally, once they were on the bus, who broke the silence.

"You know what I did this morning, Nick? I read the entire newspaper from front to back. I even read the want-ads. I seem to have . . . an enormous need to get myself back into the real world again and see what's going on." She was trying hard, Nick knew, even though her words came hesitantly. Mother sat looking out her window as the buildings flashed by. "In the help-wanted section, there was an ad for a music teacher for the St. Francis Day School."

"That's only six blocks from us," Nick put in.

"I know. I may not get it, but I'm going to apply."

"That's great, Mom. I'm really glad."

Nick leaned back against the seat and thought about what he would bring to his father the next time they came. A jar of cashews, maybe; some fancy apples; perhaps a book of *Doonesbury* cartoons. He wondered if his dad would like the cartoons or whether he would read all sorts of messages in them.

Then let him, he decided finally, closing his eyes. *I can't be responsible for everything. I can't . . . really be responsible for him at all.* It was a new thought, even though it seemed perfectly obvious. He could be concerned, he could be supportive, but he could not be responsible. He repeated it to himself again and felt a relief he had not known for some time.

He was going to have to live with ups and downs, Nick discovered after dinner. Supper had been a particularly warm, relaxed occasion, and he had felt, when he got up from the table, that the hardest part was over. But then, in his room later, with *Yesterday's Hit Tunes* on his stereo, Nick listened to the lyrics of "Cat's in the Cradle," and it was like another sock in the stomach:

> *"When you comin' home, Dad?"*
> *"I don't know when,*
> *but we'll get together then;*
> *you know we'll have a good time then. . . ."*

He let the tears come. Forced them out, in fact, until he was sure there were none left, for now anyway. It helped. Maybe things were better for his father, too. Maybe Jacob would feel that being separated from his family was punishment enough, and the Communists would go back to spying on someone else. Maybe up there on the ward in his green army pajamas, Jacob Karpinski would find a certain peace that he could not feel at home, and his fears would let him rest. Whether they did or not, there was nothing Nick could do to change matters. It was time to concentrate on things he could do something about—his own life.

He got up suddenly and washed his face. Then he went downstairs and over to the Zimmerman apartment. Karen answered the door.

Nick smiled at her. "What's a nice girl like you doing home on a Saturday night?" he said. "Come on out."

Laughing, Karen got her jacket and followed him into the hall.

"Mother will be eternally grateful," she told him.

"I'm not doing this for your mother, I'm doing it for me," Nick said as they went on down. It had begun raining outside, however, and they stood in the doorway watching the new leaves of the birch trees shiver beneath the large drops.

"Well," Nick said, "we could go for a walk in the rain or run down to the deli for cheesecake, or you could come up to our apartment. . . ."

"I'll take number three," Karen told him.

They went back inside, crossed the lobby, and started up the stairs where Nick could hear, from the rooms above, the hesitant strains of a Chopin polonaise.